ALTERNITY
DARK·MATTER adventure
the KILLING JAR
bruce r. cordell

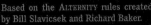

Editing: Michele Carter

Typesetting: Angelika Lokotz

Cover Art: Ashley Wood

Interior Art: Adam Rex, Ashley Wood

Cartography: Rob Lazzaretti

Graphic Design: Matt Adelsperger

Art Director: Dawn Murin

Creative Director: Richard Baker

Playtesters: Duane Maxwell, Richard Baker, JD Wiker, Andy Collins, Jeff Quick, Julia Martin

Based on the ALTERNITY rules created by Bill Slavicsek and Richard Baker.

Sources for this product include the DARK•MATTER *Campaign Setting* by Wolfgang Baur with Monte Cook, and *Mother Earth, Father Sky: Native American Myth* by Tom Lowenstein and Piers Vitebsky (Time-Life Books). Many cave room names and terms were borrowed from Wind Cave and other popular caves.

U.S., CANADA, ASIA, PACIFIC, & LATIN AMERICA
Wizards of the Coast, Inc.
P.O. Box 707
Renton, WA 98057-0707
+1-800-6324-49

EUROPEAN HEADQUARTERS
Wizards of the Coast, Belgium
P.B. 2031
2600 Berchem
Belgium
+32-70-23-32-77

VISIT OUR WEBSITE AT
www.wizards.com

Join other fans of the ALTERNITY game by joining the ALTERNITY mailing list. To join, send an email to listserv@oracle.wizards.com with the words "subscribe alternity-L" in the body of the message or "subscribe darkmatter-L" for players specifically interested in the DARK•MATTER Campaign Setting.

Introduction

"Death was in him, under him;
the earth itself was uncertain, unreliable."

--Ursula K. Le Guin, The Dispossessed

Welcome to *The Killing Jar*, an adventure set in the DARK•MATTER universe of conspiracy and horror. Xenoform sightings are more than just the ravings of madmen, pharmaceutical companies routinely violate all ethical taboos, and the deep earth covers things best left buried. Here, the heroes will discover that their worst suspicions fall short of the real, terrible truth.

What Do You Need to Play?

The Killing Jar is suitable for three to six moderately equipped heroes of any levels. As always, low-level heroes should be cautious about facing every challenge head-on. Of course, research and caution are invaluable allies for all heroes. If the heroes' average level is greater than 5th, the Gamemaster may want to augment straightforward encounters by adding d4 additional guard dogs, thugs, handlers, or other threats to each appropriate encounter.

The adventure is designed for the DARK•MATTER™ setting of the ALTERNITY® science fiction roleplaying game. To make best use of *The Killing Jar,* you'll need the ALTERNITY *Player's Handbook* (TSR 2800), the ALTERNITY *Gamemaster Guide* (TSR 2801), and the DARK•MATTER campaign book (TSR11433). A standard road atlas could also prove useful as players (and GMs) plan their characters' route.

Using This Adventure

Read the adventure before play to familiarize yourself with the outline of events. *The Killing Jar* is organized into two acts. The Lexicon of Terms included later in this chapter provides information the heroes can uncover at any time during the adventure. The Final Wrap at the end of Act Two provides the Gamemaster with several ways to conclude the adventure, as well as possible repercussions of the preceding events.

Text that appears in *italics* is meant to be paraphrased or read aloud to the players, representing information the heroes acquire through simple observation. Text within a boxed sidebar calls out important information to the GM, including special instructions, new item descriptions, and newspaper clippings. Where appropriate, the first appearance of important names or places is in SMALL CAPS, indicating that the Lexicon has additional information on the highlighted term.

Generally speaking, the information presented in the text attempts to paint broad strokes, while now and again presenting narrow, specific information on topics associated with the plot. The latter material can aid the GM in injecting additional realism into the game. For instance, while it doesn't matter one iota to the plot that a parade and fireworks occur offstage during a festival called the STERNWHEEL REGATTA, such information colorfully describes the setting, which in turn goes a long way toward providing a realistic atmosphere that can enhance gameplay.

Plot Synopsis & Background

A case of grand theft auto quickly escalates into a serious investigation leading heroes to a tow lot, a forensics lab, and finally to POINT PLEASANT, West Virginia. Sidestepping covert agents of AMERICAN HOME DEVICES, INC. (AHD) and an outbreak of a strange bacterial infection (tentatively called *CLOSTRIDIUM CNIDARAE* or *C. CNIDARAE*), the heroes encounter the MOTHMAN of Point Pleasant and discover the thief was no simple felon. Clues left by the deceased thief and evidence uncovered in Point Pleasant eventually leads the investigation to a research laboratory owned by AHD.

An innocent front hides sinister research in AHD's lower laboratories. The company is responsible for the appearance of *C. cnidarae* as part of covert biological weapons research, but AHD is not the source of the bacteria. Apparently, AHD retrieved its biosamples from below the earth, by way of MAMMOTH CAVE NATIONAL PARK in Kentucky.

The heroes discover that unexplored sections of Mammoth Cave are longer than the mapped sections by at least one order of magnitude. Furthermore, clear evidence indicates ancient Native Americans explored the cave system over 2,000 years ago. Most importantly, mothmen live in the dim tunnels, but not alone. . . . Only perseverance reveals the mothmen's presence and objectives, and the horrible truth behind *C. cnidarae*'s source.

Getting the Heroes Involved

In this adventure, success is measured by the heroes' ability to track disparate clues to the final encounter. The GM must invest the heroes in the plot—why do they care enough to handle the situation themselves?

In this case, the answer is simple: Something belonging to the PCs is stolen, and in recovering it they find both mystery and terrible danger.

The Setup

Whether the PC group is affiliated with the Hoffmann Institute or is a collection of fringe thinkers, mercenaries, and conspiracy theorists, the same plot hook applies: The car of one of the heroes is stolen, seemingly a random theft. Worse luck, compromising items and/or classified case files stored in the car are also gone! When the heroes retrieve their car, they discover that the thief left some very interesting materials behind. If the heroes are out of the country, on another case, or otherwise preoccupied, they may not even realize that the car is missing until a phone call from the West Virginia State Police reveals that the car has been recovered (see "Adventure Trigger" below).

The heroes' geographical location in the continental U.S. is important to pulling off this option. Ideally, the heroes live in or are visiting a location somewhere along I-64 in a limited range east of Frankfort and west of Charleston. This option works best if the heroes are attending a conference in Lexington (perhaps a MUFON

Railroading the PCs

The Gamemaster may be reluctant to propel the heroes into the adventure in such a manner, or other circumstances may make it impossible for the PCs to be drawn into the plot through the theft of their vehicle. In this case, the heroes receive an anonymous tip regarding an abandoned car, and are urged to check it out. The plot should progress normally from there, with the exception that JANE SCARBOROUGH (the car thief, see below) drove her own vehicle on her harrowing trip through Kentucky and West Virginia.

conference, or some other activity the GM finds appropriate) when their car is stolen. If this adventure follows naturally from a previous one of the GM's devising, it will feel more convincing and less forced to the players.

Adventure Trigger

The heroes receive a call concerning the stolen car from the HURRICANE, W. VA. police. A police operator calls the PCs approximately 24 hours after the theft. The license plates allowed the police to get the heroes' phone number, if the car was not reported stolen.

"Your car has been recovered, and it's drivable. You have fourteen days to retrieve it—it's sitting in a tow lot in Hurricane, West Virginia."

The operator provides a plausible explanation for the car's theft, if asked:

"Small-time criminals and pushers often steal cars, drive them for a while, conduct illicit activity (such as a drug deal), then abandon them. If any evidence of such activity had been found in the car, you would be unable to reclaim it for quite some time, but, like most such cases, the car is superficially clean and can be returned to its rightful owner."

When the heroes wish to pick up the car, proceed to Act One, Scene One.

Car Theft Sequence of Events
Or, Whatever Happened to Jane Scarborough?

The heroes are not initially privy to this information, but for the GM's edification an important sequence of events is presented below.

- Jane Scarborough, a research scientist employed by American Home Devices, Inc., worked for the company's pharmaceuticals division in SHELBYVILLE, KY., for years. Intrigued by the alien biologies involved in her research, she assembled her own private library of associated topics, including the mothman sightings at Point Pleasant, the curse of CHIEF CORNSTALK, and the speculative work of DR. VERNON SHABBIR.

- Early the previous week, Jane realized AHD's intent to sell the alien *C. cnidarae* organism as a biowarfare agent. She began to gather her notes and evidence, intending to take the materials to the authorities. Unfortunately, AHD discovered her intentions before she could act.

- Hoping for a quick resolution, Jane's supervisor deliberately set a trap to infect her in a way that would look like a lab accident: He placed a contaminated needle at her workstation. Thursday morning, Jane felt the needle pierce her hand and immediately realized what happened, and that she only had perhaps a few hours to follow her thin trail of evidence to a possible cure. Moving quickly, she injected a lab mouse with the *C. cnidarae* organism as proof of AHD's wrongdoing and left the building.

- During a brief stop at home, Jane called Dr. Shabbir and had him fax a map of the area reputed to hold Chief Cornstalk's burial mound. She told him she'd meet him there and started out for Point Pleasant by way of I-64 east, stopping in Lexington around noon to ditch her car at a hotel parking lot and steal another in the hope of offsetting possible pursuit.

- She drove the car along I-64 into West Virginia. Soon after crossing the border, Jane turned north onto Route 2, which follows the winding Ohio River, to Point Pleasant, W. Va. At this point, the time was 4:00 P.M.

- In Point Pleasant, Jane contacted Dr. Shabbir by phone, then made a solitary trip to the "TNT" AREA (as described in Act One, Scene Three). Because of her growing delirium, Jane left the area before Shabbir arrived or she accomplished her goal. She drove away around 5:00 P.M.

- Using back roads, Jane headed south, finally reaching I-64 again in the dead of night. She turned onto I-64, heading west at Exit 44. Deteriorating mental acuity and problems with vision forced her from the car near Hurricane, W. Va. (near Exit 34), at around 7:00 P.M. She continued west along I-64 on foot for another 9.5 kilometers before collapsing (near Exit 28), dead, at about 1:00 A.M. Friday.

- The body was reported and recovered by the police at 2:00 A.M., 14 hours after the car was stolen. AHD agent BALANCE, disguised as a CDC agent, arrived within the hour. His influence insured that the body was sent to a facility of his choosing and that the press didn't hear about the story until late Friday afternoon.

- The stolen car was recovered by the Hurricane Towing Company 18 hours after the theft. If the car belongs to the PCs, they receive a call from the police at noon on Friday, 24 hours after the theft.

- A brief report about the mysterious body by the roadside (see "An Intriguing Coincidence" in Act One, Scene One, below) appears in the Saturday morning newspaper.

Lexicon of Terms

The Lexicon is an encyclopedia-style resource. It is a compilation of general information heroes may discover during the course of this adventure. One or more information sources and the difficulty of acquiring the data from each source accompany each entry. Listed below are the available sources of information and the skill(s) most appropriate for getting information from the source. Heroes conducting research find the associated information in the indicated source by making a successful skill check. Unless otherwise indicated, a skill check carries no situation die modifier based on the nature of the information being sought (although other conditions may call for a bonus or a penalty to be applied to the check). Some Lexicon entries (such as "Lundicyx") mention a skill rather than a source of information, indicating personal knowledge a hero may have that enables him or her to access the information without recourse to research.

Source	Applicable Skills
Civil records	Investigate–*research*
Dictionary	No check required
Internet	Computer Science–*hacking,* Knowledge–*computer operation* (+1 step penalty), or Street Smart–*net savvy*
Library	Investigate–*research*
Newspaper	Investigate–*research*
Online phone directory	Computer Science–*hacking,* Knowledge–*computer operation* (+1 step penalty) or Street Smart–*net savvy*
Phone book	Investigate–*research*
Privileged*	Investigate–*research*

* Secret information that requires access to Hoffmann Institute (or similar conspiracy-savvy) databases.

American Home Devices, Inc. (AHD). See Act Two, Scene One for research details.

Balance, Andrew. Only direct investigation by the heroes possibly reveals this name as an American Home Devices, Inc. (AHD) agent attempting to cover up and erase the embarrassing appearance of the body, confuse the police by posing as a CDC agent, and derail the heroes at every step. Agent Balance's primary directive is to make certain that AHD's activities and the consequences of such activities (the body, for example) remain hidden.

CDC. Everyone knows "CDC" stands for the Centers for Disease Control and Prevention, an agency of the U.S. Department of Health and Human Services. For public information about the agency, visit the CDC's website at <http://www.cdc.gov/>. Initially, the CDC is not even really involved with this case, though at the DM's option, too much interference on the heroes' part could precipitate a covert CDC investigation. "Wrap-up: Act One, Scene One" describes the role (or lack thereof) of the CDC in this adventure.

Also: [Privileged source, no modifier; Lore–*conspiracy theories* skill check, +1 step penalty] See the DARK•MATTER campaign book "CDC" entry for the various rumors about the agency.

Charleston, W. Va. See Act One, Scene Three.

Also: [Lore–*UFO lore* skill check, no modifier] On Tuesday, March 11, 1997, at 6:30 P.M., three unidentified orange spheres appeared over the south bank of the Kanawha River, in the South Hills section of Charleston, West Virginia. This sighting is a red herring in regard to the adventure, but inquisitive heroes (and creative Gamemasters) may make of it what they will.

Clostridium cnidarae [Clo•*strih*•de•um *Nih*•dar•ay]. See Act One, Scene Two, F11 and Act Two, Scene Two, room P24.

Also: [Internet source, no modifier; Life Science–*biology* skill check, +2 step penalty]: No such microorganism has yet been classified in accepted official listings; however, microorganisms exist with similar names, including *Clostridium histolyticum* and *Clostridium perfringens.* Interestingly enough, these parasites produce a substance called collagenase that breaks down collagen, the framework of muscles, a process that facilitates gas gangrene. By itself, the word "cnidarae" could refer to the Phylum Cnidaria, which contains a number of creatures including jellyfish and the freshwater hydra. Cnidarians have only two layers of living tissues separated by a gelatinous layer. All cnidarians have stinging nematocysts that function in prey capture. Tentacles with nematocysts surround the mouth, which is the only opening to the digestive system.

Supporting Cast

Listed below are the page numbers where statistics for supporting cast members and primary threats may be found, in order of appearance.

Regional Map

INDIANA

OHIO

I-77

Point Pleasant

Charleston

Louisville

Shelbyville

Hurricane

I-64

WEST VIRGINIA

Lexington

KENTUCKY

I-65

Mammoth Cave National Park

VIRGINIA

0 18 36 54 72
kilometers

Cnidocyte, Secondary [*Nih•doh•site*]. See Act Two, Scene Two, room P24.

Cnidocyte, Tertiary. See Act Two, Scene Two, room P24.

Cornstalk, Chief. See Act One, Scene Three.

Also: [Internet source, +1 step penalty; Library source, +2 step penalty; Lore–*occult lore* skill check, +2 step penalty] The Curse of Chief Cornstalk: During the mid 1700s the first white men settled the area now known as Point Pleasant, West Virginia. The area had long been the home of the Shawnee, led by Chief Cornstalk. A charismatic figure, Cornstalk stood an imposing (for the time) nearly 2 meters tall. He was a gifted speaker who could "stir men's souls" with his orations. Cornstalk led his people in a military attempt to drive out the settlers.

Long recognized as the decisive engagement in a protracted series of Indian wars, the Battle of Point Pleasant is also known as the "First Battle of the Revolution." Several historians have successfully argued that "the shot heard 'round the world" was fired here and not at Lexington over six months later. The Indians, they contend, had been incited by British agents to harass the colonists and thus keep their minds off their grievances against the mother country.

When his campaign failed, Cornstalk attempted to negotiate for peace. Unfortunately, the settlers still harbored resentment over the Battle of Point Pleasant. In retaliation, disgruntled former soldiers murdered Chief Cornstalk and his young son in cold blood. Legend maintains that Chief Cornstalk placed a 200-year curse (give or take a few decades) on the town of Point Pleasant with his dying breath. Some say that the appearance of the mothman (see below) is part of this curse.

Doorway. [Privileged source, +4 step penalty] Only the most knowledgeable institutions have any inkling that the Earth harbors doorways that lead—by all best hypothesis—to other dimensions. These groups keep such information hidden, either to exploit the doorway or keep it sealed against whatever may come through, depending on their agendas. Either way, the proof of the existence and location of a doorway is an invaluable addition to the study of paranormal lore.

Kearns, Michele. [Phone book or Online phone directory source, no modifier] Address, phone number, and/or office extension provided. Michele Kearns is merely a spokesperson for the Charleston, W. Va., police, and knows nothing more about the body, AHD, mothmen, or any other mysterious knowledge pertaining to this adventure. Should the heroes manage to contact her, she refers them to the officer on site, Detective Sergeant Mark Gordon (see Act One, Scene Two).

Kline, Julius, Ph.D. See Act One, Scene Two.

Also: [Privileged source, +1 step penalty] A Dr. Kline belonged to the Wichita, KS Masonic lodge, but was expelled for unspecified reasons 10 years ago. If confronted with this knowledge, Kline only chuckles, revealing nothing.

Gordon, Mark, Detective Sergeant. See Act One, Scene Two.

Hurricane, W. Va. See Act One, Scene One.

Lundicyx. [Medical Science–*medical knowledge* skill check, no modifier] Lundicyx is a drug recommended for the treatment of insomnia in patients who have difficulty falling asleep. Lundicyx, the first in a new class of non-benzodiazepine (pyrazolopyrimidine) chemical compounds, allows people to fall asleep quickly and awaken refreshed without many of the side effects associated with other currently available sleep medications.

Also: [Medical Science–*medical knowledge* skill check, +2 step penalty] In clinical studies, Lundicyx is shown to be well tolerated. The most common side effects are headache, drowsiness, and nightmares.

Mammoth Cave. [Internet source, –1 step bonus; Library, –1 step bonus] Mammoth Cave National Park was authorized as a national park in 1926 and was fully established July 1, 1941. It was established to preserve the cave system, the scenic river valleys of the Green and Nolin rivers, and a section of the hilly country of south central Kentucky. This is the longest recorded cave system in the world, with more than 560 kilometers explored and mapped. Mammoth Cave was designated as a World Heritage Site in 1981, and as an International Biosphere Reserve in 1990. Mammoth Cave National Park has 52,830 acres.

Also: [Lore–*occult lore* skill check, +2 step penalty; Social Science–*history* skill check, +3 step penalty] In the late 1800's, a group of people tried to start a colony deep in Mammoth Cave. The colony eventually failed, but stories persist that its failure was due to the fact that the cave system was haunted.

Also: [Social Science–*anthropology* skill check, +2 step penalty]: Near the end of the Late Archaic period (3000–1000 BC) Archaic Indians began exploring Mammoth Cave and other caves in the area, collecting minerals they found. Why Late Archaic people traveled deep into Mammoth Cave to collect selenite, mirabilite, epsomite, and gypsum is a matter of speculation. The most likely reason is that these minerals were valued for their medicinal properties and/or ceremonial uses, and that they were traded to other groups for food, shells, chert, and other goods. Native legends suggest that the Archaic peoples communed with earth spirits that lived deep within the caves.

Mason, Lester. See Act One, Scene One.

McClintic Wildlife Preserve. See Act One, Scene Three.

Also: [Internet source, no modifier; Civil records source, no modifier] 3,535 acres; Mason County, W. Va. Located 8 kilometers north of Point Pleasant off state Route 62. The McClintic Preserve contains the greatest variety of wildlife habitats to be found on any of West Virginia's wildlife management Areas. Approximately 600 acres farmland, 900 acres brushland, 160 acres wetland, and 1,100 acres mixed hardwood forest combine to provide excellent hunting for deer, waterfowl, turkey, squirrel, rabbit, grouse, mourning dove, and woodcock. Nine rustic campsites with drinking water and vault toilets are available. Also see "TNT Area," below.

Mothman. See Act One, Scene Three, and Act Two, Scenes Two and Three.

Also: [Internet source, no modifier; Library, no modifier; Lore–*occult lore* skill check, no modifier] The mothmen are a species of flying, vaguely insectoid creatures most famously sighted in Point Pleasant, W. Va, in 1966 and 1967. While their haunting red eyes and huge wings leave quite an impression on eyewitnesses, those who have seen mothmen seem curiously terrorized by the sightings, suffering recurrent nightmares, flashbacks, and even insect phobias for years thereafter. This is the case even when the witnesses caught only brief or obscured glimpse of the mothman, and when they suffered no physical harm. An additional check at a +1 step penalty reveals the information presented in this Lexicon about Chief Cornstalk.

Also: [Internet source, no modifier; Library source, no modifier] Many dozens of firsthand witness accounts of mothman sightings can be found including the following:

The mothman's glowing red eyes were first reported on November 14, 1966, in Salem, West Virginia. That evening, Newell Partridge was watching television at his home. The following is his account:

"It was about 10:30 that night, and suddenly the TV blanked out. A real fine herringbone pattern appeared on the tube, and at the same time the set started a loud whining noise. It sounded like a generator winding up.

"The dog was sitting on the end of the porch, howling down toward the hay barn.

"I shined the [flash] light in that direction, and it picked up two red circles, or eyes, which looked like bicycle reflectors.

"I certainly know what animal eyes look like; these were much larger. It's a good length of a football field to that hay barn. Still, those eyes showed up huge for that distance. It was an eerie feeling. I have never had this sort of feeling before. It was as if you knew something was wrong, but couldn't place just what it was."

Partridge described the intense, morbid fear that swept over him as a "cold chill." The dog snarled and ran toward the eyes, but Newell hurried inside. He slept with his shotgun all night. The next day, he and his six-year-old son went searching for the dog, Bandit, a large, muscular German shepherd. Those tracks were going in a circle, as if the dog had been chasing his tail, though he never did that. There were no other tracks of any kind. Bandit was never seen again.

Nematocyst [Nem•*ah*•toe•sist]. [Internet source, no modifier; Dictionary, automatic] A capsule containing a barbed threadlike tube that delivers a paralyzing sting.

New Madrid Earthquake. See Act Two, Scene Two, P24. For more information (not necessary for this adventure), see the following informative website: <http://asms.k12.ar.us/armem/richards/index.htm>.

Pellucidar. [Internet source, no modifier; Library source, no modifier; Knowledge–*literature* skill check, no modifier] *At The Earth's Core*, a work of fiction by Edgar Rice Burroughs first published in 1914, describes a vast inner world populated by a wealth of flora and fauna, including humanoid cultures.

Also: See Act Two, Scene Two. The AHD Pharmaceuticals database uses "Pellucidar" as a code name for a recently discovered cave system within Mammoth Cave.

Point Pleasant, W. Va. See Act One, Scene Three.

Also: [Internet source, no modifier; Library source, no modifier; Lore–*occult lore* skill check, no modifier] Research on Point Pleasant leads to the information presented about mothmen in this Lexicon.

Primary Source. Act Two, Scene Two, room P24.

Scarborough, Jane. [Online phone directory, no modifier] A random search for all people with this name reveals over ninety-one people possess it in the United States alone. Trying to get a fix on Jane Scarborough's prior occupation or location in this scatter-shot manner is impossible without additional triangulation techniques, such as investigation of the material provided in the adventure.

Also: Once the heroes learn, through the course of their investigation, that Jane once worked for AHD, they may call the company headquarters with questions about Jane. Such a call is quickly transferred to a brusque-sounding man (Agent Andrew Balance) who attempts to determine the reason for the heroes' interest. Should he infer that the heroes know too much, he immediately initiates a trace on the call, and may dispatch a strike force of two AHD field handlers to deal with the heroes. If Balance discovers the location of the heroes' call (heroes calling from their own cell phones may not be *immediately* traceable), the heroes' real names become known to Balance, who begins to use their real names at the next opportunity.

[Phone book or Online phone directory, no modifier] Jane's home address and phone number are easily located, but of course, no one is home.

Shabbir, Dr. See Act One, Scene Three.

Also: [Online phone directory, no modifier; Point Pleasant Phone book, automatic] Chiropractor's Office at 1710 Jefferson Blvd, Point Pleasant WV 25550. (No private listing)

Also: [Lore–*occult lore* skill check, +1 step penalty] A Vernon Shabbir is the author of several self-published books that make an assortment of claims, but whose central theme is that archaic peoples of North America had real contact with spiritual entities.

Silver Bridge. [Internet source, +1 step penalty; Social Science–*history* skill check, +2 step penalty] Fifty-two people lost their lives when the Silver Bridge collapsed in 1967. The official cause of failure is listed as eyebar fracture and inadequate inspection.

Also: [Lore–*conspiracy theories* or *occult lore* skill check, +1 step penalty] Many conspiracy theorists suspect Chief Cornstalk's ancient curse precipitated the failure of the Silver Bridge.

Smithy, Jon. This alias accompanies the email address <devermis@yahoo.com>. Only direct hero investigation during the course of the adventure may reveal the name behind this alias: AHD agent Andrew Balance.

Sternwheel. [Dictionary, automatic] A flat-bottomed steamboat propelled by a paddlewheel at the stern (rear).

Sternwheel Regatta. [Newspaper source, no modifier; Internet source, no modifier] A four-day festival in Point Pleasant, W. Va., involving a variety of entertainments, including steamboat races. The Regatta usually takes place in June, but the GM can adjust the timing of this event to suit the campaign.

Teroic Pseudonucleic Acid (TPA). [Privileged source, +3 step penalty; Lore–*UFO lore* skill check, +4 step penalty] Scientists have discovered another genetic foundation for life aside from Terran DNA: teroic pseudonucleic acid (TPA). The TPA forms are all much more closely related to one another genetically than DNA lifeforms. This could mean that they are all more recently evolved (and thus have had less time to drift from their common ancestors) or it could mean that they are simply more tightly engineered to meet some universal genetic standard.

"TNT" Area. [Internet source, +1 step penalty; Civil records source, +1 step penalty] Several acres of the McClintic Wildlife Preserve were leased or sold off during World War II (to companies including Trojan-U.S. Powder Company, the LFC Chemical Company, and American Home Devices, Inc.) remain officially part of the pre-

What if Heroes Alert the Authorities?

Many times during the adventure, evidence uncovered by the heroes might prove useful to local law enforcement and related authorities. Generally speaking, alerting the authorities only limits the heroes' later options, and thus such actions should be discouraged. Hoffmann Institute employees ought to remember that agents are expected to solve their own problems without involving other agencies, and freelance investigators are often too cautious (or paranoid) to trust official law enforcement. But sometimes the best intentions go awry and the police become involved anyway.

In a best-case scenario, the player characters anonymously provide information to the authorities. When heroes provide information without disguising themselves, they run the risk of being tied up in months of legal proceedings. Worse, the police take any evidence accumulated by the heroes to further their own investigations, possibly leaving the heroes high and dry. Moreover, heroes who appear to have privileged information may become suspects themselves, especially if felony-class activities are brought to light. Two possibilities are provided here to aid the GM in ameliorating the consequences of police involvement.

First, if the heroes' information is odd or strange enough, the police label the heroes "kooks" and throw them out of the station, ignoring any further attempts by the heroes to pass on their discoveries. So much for alerting the authorities—the heroes must solve their problems on their own.

Second, the heroes' enemies (in this case, agents of American Home Devices, Inc.) may themselves help anonymously extricate the players from legal entanglements that pertain to the adventure. AHD doesn't want any hint of its activities to leak to regular law enforcement. To this end, highly placed AHD allies, agents, and resources reach down through levels of bureaucracy to conveniently lose case files, erase statements, and possibly even release suspects in any way related to their plans. Thus, heroes who have run afoul of the local police could suddenly find their present difficulty simply evaporate, at the GM's discretion. Of course, heroes released from the net of normal law enforcement might walk right into an AHD ambush.

serve, but artifacts of wartime land use remain. The most obtrusive unreclaimed area is the abandoned "TNT" area, containing empty production plants and over one hundred earth-covered storage "igloos."

Useful Sources

Many real-life sources can provide additional details to GMs who want to develop this adventure further. Note that some of the websites listed below may not be current at the time of this publication, most likely because particularly revealing websites are routinely suppressed by the conspiracy.

Books

Barker, Gray. *The Silver Bridge*
Keel, John. *The Complete Guide to Mysterious Beings*
Keel, John. *The Mothman Prophesies*

Websites

AHD:
    http://www.americanhomedevices.com
Chief Cornstalk and the Silver Bridge:
    http://members.aol.com/mothmanwww/unusual.html
Hoffmann Institute's "Public" Page:
    http://www.hoffmanninstitute.com
Indian artifacts:
    http://www2.itexas.net/~teddun/tedspage.htm
Mammoth Cave:
    Official site: http://www.nps.gov/maca/
    http://www.mammoth.cave.national-park.com/
    http://www.mammothcave.com/cavarn.htm
Mapping & local information:
    http://www.mapblast.com/mblast/index.mb
Mothman:
    http://members.aol.com/mothmanwww/index.html
    http://members.aol.com/mothmanwww/unusual.html
    http://www.fortunecity.com/victorian/rembrandt/45/ex3a.htm
    http://www.geocities.com/Area51/Cavern/7270/mothman.html
    http://www.geocities.com/SunsetStrip/Alley/7982/mothman.htm
    http://www.inergy.com/RonPowell/mothman.html
    http://www.parascope.com/en/cryptozoo/predators02.htm
    http://www.prairieghosts.com/moth.html
Sternwheel Regatta:
    http://members.aol.com/sternwheel/index.html
TNT area:
    http://members.aol.com/mothmanwww/map.html
What THEY don't want you to know:
    http://www.dangeroustoread.net

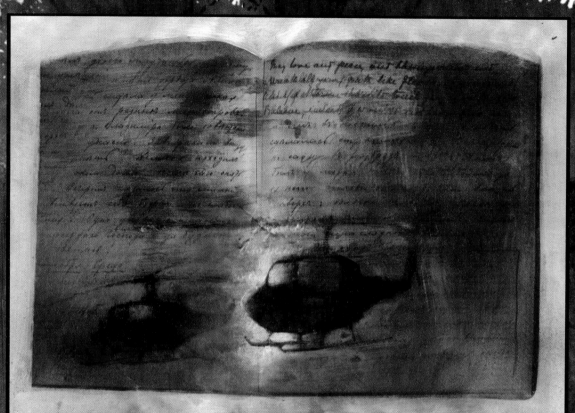

(The evil that men do lives after them,
the good is oft interred with their
bones·
--shakespeare, julius caesar iii, ii, 79)

Wherein the heroes' investigation leads them to an annual festival in Point Pleasant, a place best known for its mothman sightings.

Setting

Most of the adventure of Act One is set in the state of West Virginia, called the Mountain State (capital: Charleston). Like any large state of the union, West Virginia has many interesting cities and sights, all of which are described in great detail in any number of sources, including road atlases and online resources. However, only the most cursory information concerning West Virginia is necessary for the purposes of this adventure. Although a real atlas provides better detail, refer to the Regional Map for locations important to this act: Hurricane, Charleston, and Point Pleasant.

Scene One: Hurricane, W. Va.

Coordinates:
Lat: 38° 26' 12" N
Lon: 82° 1' 0" W
Nearest Airport: Tri-State/Milton J Ferguson Field
Population: ~4,500
Suggested Lodging: Hollywood Motel, Main St., Hurricane WV 25526.

Heroes must physically travel to Hurricane to investigate the car. The small town is typical for its size, having only a few amenities. Other than the car in the tow lot, little else concerning the town is important to the adventure, although the GM can easily develop this area if desired.

The heroes' information reveals that the car is held in impound by Hurricane Towing, owned by Lester Mason. Calls ahead of time to Mason reveal that any investigation of the car requires an impound fee of $174, at which time the car will be released. Paraphrase or read the following information when the investigators arrive at Hurricane Towing:

A slate-colored warehouse squats amid several similar, obviously abandoned buildings. Chain link fence topped with barbed wire encloses a large area adjacent to the warehouse, but slats prevent a clear view into the interior, though it's obvious that many, many cars are parked within. A sliding electrical gate closes off access to the lot proper.

The adjacent warehouse has a single exterior door, on which the words "Hurricane Towing, Office" are simply stenciled. A red tow truck is parked askew near the door, emblazoned with the same logo.

Hurricane Towing's office hours are 7 A.M. to 7 P.M. six days a week (closed on Sunday). Because Hurricane is so close to the interstate, a number of the cars have out-of-state plates. See the Hurricane Towing map on the inside front cover.

Lester Mason

Heroes who arrive during office hours can head up a short flight of steps and enter Lester Mason's small office. The office contains a computer (not linked to the Internet), a phone, a fax, a small soda dispenser vintage 1950, and a big bulletin board with pinups of all types, plus Lester's Ceredo Hurricane High School diploma (class of '87).

The tow lot operator is 29 years old. He has short-cropped black hair and a thin mustache. He's lived in Hurricane his whole life, a proud graduate of Ceredo Hurricane High School. For fun, he races his souped-up '73 VW Beetle in the local weekly derby. His best friend Sheila, a large German shepherd, patrols inside the fenced lot at night. To save on rent, Lester lives in the small room adjacent to the main office.

Lester reveals the following information if questioned:
- The heroes are welcome to claim the stolen car if they own it, as long as they pay the impound fee of $174.
- If the heroes do not own the car, they may not examine the vehicle or take anything from it if they're not the owners. He

Lester Mason

Nonprofessional

STR	11	[+1]	INT	9	[0]
DEX	9	[0]	WIL	8	[0]
CON	9		PER	8	

Durability: 9/9/5/5   Action Check: 9/4/2
Move: sprint 20, run 12, walk 4   #Actions: 2
Reaction Score: Ordinary/2   Last Resorts: 0

Attacks

Unarmed	13/6/3	d4s/d4+1s/d4+2s	LI/O
Knife	12/6/3	d4w/d4+1w/d4+2w	LI/O
Pistol, .38 rev.	12/6/3	d4w/d4+1w/d4m	HI/O

Defenses
+1 resistance modifier vs. melee attacks

Skills
Athletics [11]; Melee [11]–*blade [12]*; Unarmed [11]–*brawl [13]*; Modern [9]–*pistol [11]*; Vehicle Operation [9], Stamina [9]–*endurance [10]*; Knowledge [9]–*language: English [12]*; Technical [9]–*juryrig [10]*, Awareness [8]; Street Smart [8]; Interaction [8]–*intimidate [10]*.

Gear
.38 revolver, concealed holster, knife, mini-tool kit, lighter, keychain laser pointer.

might, however, be agreeable to a bribe. . . . His price to claim that the car was stolen from the lot begins at $350, though he can be negotiated down to $275 through successful use of the Interaction–*bargain* skill (at a +2 step penalty). In either case, the price is sufficient to release the car (at which time the heroes can search it at their leisure).

- With a successful Interaction check by the heroes, Lester reveals that Hurricane police found the car on I-64, on the Kentucky–West Virginia border. As is usual for abandoned cars with no evidence of apparent criminal activity, the police called the nearest tow service for retrieval, simple as that. The car was found in the westbound lane, just west of Exit 34.

Surreptitious Investigation

Heroes who do not wish to pay the impound fee after talking with Lester, or who do not wish to deal with Lester at all, may decide merely to break into the impound lot. Breaking in during the day draws instant attention from passing motorists and other nearby observers. The best opportunity to break in is during the concealing cover of night.

The office is protected by two standard locks, one to the building proper, and one at the top of the flight of stairs leading from the outside door. Bypassing the locks requires a successful Manipulation–*lockpick* check. Once in the office, the least dexterous hero present must make a Stealth check once per minute to avoid waking Lester, who is sleeping in the next room. If Lester wakes,

he first calls 911 from his adjacent room, then confronts the "thieves" with his pistol. Heroes accurately identified by Lester are later listed in police blotters as casual thieves; however, heroes who harm or slay Lester are felons, and are hounded by regular law enforcement for years to come!

A successful Investigate–*search* check reveals the following items: keys to the security system protecting the lot (see below) and a picture of the car to be investigated matched with plates (useful for identifying the car in the lot if the heroes do not own it).

An alarm and an electrified fence (automatically inflicts 2s [En/O] per contact/per phase) protect the main tow lot. A large German shepherd named Sheila also patrols the interior of the lot at night. Casual attempts at entry result in electrical shock and the activation of the blaring alarm. The alarm alerts both Sheila (who arrives in 2 rounds) and Lester (arrives in 5 rounds). Neither are amenable to thieves in the night, and they defend their turf to the best of their abilities. Lester also calls the local police if the alarm sounds, and they arrive on site in 15 minutes (use the police statistics provided in Act Two, Scene Two for average police officers).

Deactivating the electrical fence and alarm is automatic if the heroes recover the proper keys from Lester's office (see above). Otherwise, deactivation requires two successful Security–*security devices* checks. A failure for the alarm sets it off, while a failure for the electrical fence automatically inflicts 5s (En/O) on the active hero.

The Car

The heroes' car is drivable, though the steering column is broken; the car can be easily started with a screwdriver. About a quarter-tank of gas remains.

Items the PCs left in the car are still there, though these items have obviously been rifled through. A few new things catch their attention: A small plastic container lies discarded in the back seat, a purse nestles beneath the driver's seat, and a carton half filled with Marlboro cigarettes lies on the floor in the back seat. Even a particularly thorough search may not divulge the organism growing inside the driver-side seat stuffing (see below).

The nondescript purse holds a variety of common oddments including lip balm, a comb, a pen, aspirin, makeup, and sunglasses. It holds no checks, credit cards, driver's license, or other identifications—except for an unmarked magnetic security card. The purse also contains a few unused kerchiefs, each with the initials J.S. stitched upon them. This clue ties this car to the newspaper clipping noted below, which in turn directs heroes to investigate Scene Two of this act.

The magnetic security card found in the purse is emblazoned only with the numbers 11636 37424. The card allows entry into secure spaces in the AHD facility described in Act Two; hopefully, the heroes hold onto it. Without any other identifying mark, there is no way to track down this magnetic card from the millions of similar cards sold by a variety of manufacturers to companies concerned with security.

A miniature tracking device is snagged in the side of the purse, though this is not obvious unless the heroes carefully inspect the purse (a successful Investigate–*search* check). The company makes

Sheila, German Shepherd

STR	11	[+1]	INT	3	(Animal 11)
DEX	11	[+1]	WIL	12	
CON	9		PER	3	(Animal 11)

Durability: 9/9/5/5
Move: sprint 56, run 36, walk 10
Reaction Score: Ordinary/2

Action Check: 14+/13/6/3
#Actions: 3
Last Resorts: 0

Attacks

Bite	13/6/3	d6s/d4w/d4+2w	LI/O

Defenses

+1 resistance modifier vs. melee attacks
+1 resistance modifier vs. ranged attacks
Armor: d4–2 (LI), none (HI), none (En)

Skills

Stealth [11]–*shadow [12]*; Movement [9]–*race [10]*; Stamina [9]–*endurance [12]*; Awareness [12]–*intuition [15]*, *perception [13]*; Investigate [12]–*track [16]*; Resolve [12]–*physical [13]*.

Sheila stands 1 meter high at the shoulder and is completely loyal to Lester Mason. Sheila defends the tow lot to her best ability.

a habit of "tagging" employees who work in sensitive facilities, and the transmitter allows any AHD agent within 48 kilometers to find the purse. Unfortunately for the heroes, if they take the purse with them, Agent Balance keeps tabs on the heroes' location and general movements from now on.

Heroes who have the ability or resources to analyze the bug (which requires an electronics lab) learn that the transmission range is 48 kilometers, but the components are clean and advanced black-box technology (it can't be traced to a manufacturer). See "Wrap-up: Act One, Scene One" for further development.

Patches of a strange residue, perhaps dried mucus or gel, stain the plastic container. If the heroes have any way to analyze the crusty white powder (either by sending it to an affiliate lab via Federal Express, or doing the analysis themselves in a mobile lab), an average science or forensic lab can enable a hero to determine that the substance is organic, but contaminated with very odd chemical signatures. No evidence of a pathogen is indicated. A Hoffmann Institute lab (or one owned by a similarly "in-the-know" organization) determines that the organic material contains TEROIC PSEUDONU-CLEIC ACID (TPA), indicating possible extraterrestrial origins; however, the lab is unable to provide additional information at this time. Note that the closest large Hoffmann Institute office is the Chicago branch, about a 5-hour drive away, though heroes could still send the Hoffmann lab a specimen via overnight delivery.

If the heroes dust for prints or have the car dusted for prints,

they find one clear set on the door handle (Lester Mason's), and many peculiar sets on the back of the mirror, steering wheel, and purse. The whorls and ridges are strangely smeared and melted and do not provide sufficient information to match them to any known print.

Investigators who think to check the odometer and match it against the last known reading (a Knowledge–*deduce* check), find that a total of 346 additional kilometers have been driven. This mirrors Jane Scarborough's trip from Lexington to Point Pleasant and finally to Hurricane as described in the "Car Theft Sequence of Events" in the Introduction.

The plastic container once held Jane's proof of a monstrous conspiracy: a TERTIARY CNIDOCYTE. Before she fled the AHD lab, she secretly injected a mouse with the *cnidarae* organism. Unless the heroes specifically remove the seat from the car and tear out all the stuffing, they have little chance of finding the organism before it makes its presence known on its own.

If the heroes use the stolen car during their investigations in the region, the attack occurs within 1d4 hours after the heroes retrieve the vehicle, or at another time as determined by the GM. (For example, during a late-night drive, as the cnidocyte bursts out the rear of the seat to attack a back-seat passenger.) If for some reason they decide not to take the car, the cnidocyte attacks them immediately as they examine the vehicle in the tow lot.

This tertiary cnidocyte is smaller than the one described in Act One, Scene Two, F13. It resembles an aggressive, land-dwelling jellyfish, if such a thing existed. When this cnidocyte specimen perishes, it dries up into a powdery residue similar to that found in the purse. Heroes who suffer damage from the creature's attack stand the chance of being infected with *C. cnidarae* as noted below. A hero infected with this disease could provide a powerful incentive to see the adventure to its end, in hopes for a cure.

An unexpected encounter with this cnidocyte is a good way to motivate heroes uninterested in investigation or too paranoid to follow all the leads, apart from the wonderful horror it evokes in surprised players.

An Intriguing Coincidence

Present the players with the following news clipping, either provided by the Institute or gathered from the PCs' casual perusal of the paper while the heroes are physically retrieving their car. (Allow the heroes an Awareness–*perception* check to notice the piece in the local paper, on the radio, or from an online news service.)

The police have not yet connected the body with the abandoned car. The body is that of Jane Scarborough, who stole the heroes' car and drove the vehicle until she become too disoriented to continue driving. From that point (along I-64, near Hurricane, W. Va.), Jane walked through the night, delirious, until she perished due to her strange condition: a *C. cnidarae* infection.

If the heroes are not provided with the link between the car and the body, or if the evidence supplied from the car is not sufficient for the heroes to make the connection with the preceding news story, a successful Knowledge–*deduce* check at a –1 step bonus provides the mental connection.

Tertiary Cnidocyte

STR	4	(d4+2)	INT	2	(Animal 7 or d4+5)
DEX	10	(d8+6)	WIL	6	(d4+4)
CON	10	(d8+6)	PER	7	(Animal 7 or d4+5)

Durability: 10/10/5/5   Action check: 9+/8/4/2
Move: undulate 6   #Actions: 2
Reaction Score: Marginal/1   Last Resorts: 0
Special: Only completely killed if burned. "Slain" cnidocytes otherwise recover full health in 10 days.

Attacks

Nematocyst sting* (×3)	10/5/2	1s/d4s/d4w	LI/O

    * Sting: At the end of any conflict in which a hero has taken any direct damage from a cnidocyte, the victim must make a CON feat check at a +1 step penalty. Those who fail the check become infected with *C. cnidarae;* refer to the sidebar labeled "*C. cnidarae* Contamination" for onset time and symptoms.

Defenses

–2 resistance modifier vs. melee attacks
Armor: d6–3 (LI), d6–2 (HI), d4–2 (En)

Skills

Stealth [10]–*sneak [11];* Stamina [10]–*endurance [11];* Awareness [6]–*intuition [10].*

C. cnidarae Contamination

Heroes contaminated with *C. cnidarae* through a cnidocyte's sting or deliberate "poisoning" must make a CON feat check at a +1 step penalty to avoid infection. On a failed check, the hero is infected, though no immediate symptoms manifest. Note that this "disease" does not progress according to standard infections, and thus is not modeled exactly as disease is presented in the *Gamemaster Guide*; unfortunately, an infected hero has no chance of spontaneously fighting off the infection without the specific cure. Nothing short of the specific cure in the possession of the mothmen (see Act Two) prevents the victim from perishing.

C. cnidarae and its effects accumulate as follows. Symptoms from previous days remain in effect as new symptoms occur.

Days Since Infection	Symptoms
2d4	None; incubation period (IP)
IP+1	Minute boils on skin (Awareness–*perception* check to notice)
IP+2	Runny nose, sore throat
IP+3	Fatigue (if fatigue points are used, victim is debited 1 while infection lasts)
IP+4	Occasional blurred vision (+1 step penalty to *perception* checks)
IP+5	Occasional spells of "the shakes" (+1 step penalty to STR- and DEX-based skills)
IP+6	Mental fatigue (+1 step penalty to INT- and WIL-based skills)
IP+12	Mental deterioration (additional +2 step penalty to INT- and WIL-based skills)
IP+13	Skin becomes flaccid and minute patches slough away, leaving jellylike residue*.
IP+16	Mental break; character becomes dangerously forgetful (50%) or sociopathic (50%).
IP+18	Victim succumbs as body completes liquefaction from inside out, turning translucent.
IP+18+1d4	Translucent cadaver completes its transformation into an active SECONDARY CNIDOCYTE** (see Act Two).

* Casual contact with sloughed skin is safe, unless ingested or somehow injected into the bloodstream. Such action demands an immediate CON feat check at a +1 step penalty to avoid infection.

** During AHD's development of an enzyme accelerant designed to speed up the course of the infection to a matter of hours instead of days, many researchers were contaminated with precursor enzymes, including Jane Scarborough. Should a compromised AHD researcher become infected with *C. cnidarae*, the disease runs its course in just 2d12 hours. Unfortunately, the trace contamination isn't sufficiently large to prevent final cnidocyte transformation, as is the case for a full dose of the accelerant.

BODY FOUND ALONG I-64

CHARLESTON, WV. (Reuters) — Investigators worked through the night to identify the body of a woman found early Friday morning along I-64, several kilometers west of Charleston, near Exit 28. Police spokesperson Michele Kearns said the unidentified woman's body was undergoing forensic examination and investigators hoped to establish a positive identification soon.

"At this time the identity of the body has still not been established," Kearns said in a statement. Though identification has not been established, the police reported the initials J.S. appeared on a handkerchief.

Concern existed that the death involved infectious agents. "Thankfully, it looks like undiagnosed pneumonia was the culprit," said Kearns, based on the observations of a Centers for Disease Control (CDC) field agent on site.

Police have thus far declined to comment on any possible suspects and no arrests have been made. "Though tragic, it appears this death occurred through natural causes," say police.

Wrap-up: Act One, Scene One

If all goes well, the heroes recover the purse that links the stolen car with the body found recently along I-64 to the east. At this point, the heroes may decide to investigate the body directly, if they have not already done so. Refer to Scene Two of this act.

Particularly paranoid heroes may want to stay clear of the police, and thus miss out on the adventure presented in the police forensics lab of Act One, Scene Two. If the game begins to stall in this fashion, the GM can use Hoffmann Institute membership (or a group affiliation of your choice), to spur the PCs along.

The information passed along to the heroes is sparse. Basically, the PCs must investigate a story concerning the discovery of a body along a highway, and learn why the CENTERS FOR DISEASE CONTROL AND PREVENTION (CDC) is involved (as revealed in the news clipping above). Any leads are to be followed up, and if possible, resolved. **GM Note:** Agents of the CDC are not really present in this adventure—their involvement is a sham cooked up by American Home Devices, Inc.

It's also possible that one of the heroes has been infected with *C. cnidarae*, which could drive the plot forward by itself (as the PCs search to find a cure before it's too late). Neither the heroes' own medical expertise, if any, nor a visit to a hospital or other health care center is able to cure an infected hero. Simple blood biopsies show trace amounts of collagenase, while skin biopsies show active specimens of an unknown large macro-organism (luckily, *C. cnidarae* is not infectious except through direct blood transfusion).

A common hospital doctor is at a loss to explain the symptoms or to identify the strange hydralike organisms, but recommends the infected hero stay for observation. Unfortunately, every day of inactivity brings the infected hero closer to death. Worse, the medical facility will quarantine the hero and call the CDC.

Due to Agent Balance's efforts, the Centers for Disease Control is unaware of the fruit of AHD's research. If the CDC (closest CDC office: Morgantown, W. Va.) is contacted by concerned hospital staff (or if the heroes inform the CDC outright!), there is a danger that this adventure could spiral off in a direction where the heroes become minimally involved, if not completely left out. (The CDC's primary concern is the detection of threatening disease vectors, especially those of exceptional origin.)

A few methods offer themselves to the GM who would rather keep the CDC out of the picture.

First, any hero with an affiliation or contact with the Hoffmann Institute can make a Knowledge–*deduce* check to remember that while the Institute has a generally friendly relationship with the CDC, agents should be wary of sharing too much information with this nationally funded organization. A successful Lore–*conspiracy theories* check identifies the same concerns described above.

Second, AHD has gone to a lot of effort at planting secret agents within the CDC precisely in order to hide any suspicious findings of its illicit research. Even if samples of *C. cnidarae* are directly sent to the CDC, an AHD plant receives it and quietly disposes of it, while at the same time alerting Agent Balance to the sender's address to deal with the heroes personally.

Third, the CDC may actually be compromised at the highest levels, and the organization is fully aware of AHD's secret efforts. In this scenario, the CDC responds in the same manner described above (ignoring hero claims, but dispatching Balance to the heroes' last known location immediately).

Bugged?

Heroes who inadvertently acquire the purse, complete with an electronic bug originally tagged for Jane Scarborough, draw AHD attention. Specifically, Agent Balance is periodically aware of their location, and may bedevil the heroes' efforts at specific times, as indicated by triggers in the text called out by the word "Bugged?"

Above and beyond the keyed responses dictated in the adventure, bugged heroes are also beset by periodic thug attacks (one attack every d4+2 days) aimed at them by Agent Balance. Even if heroes do nothing to advance the plot of the adventure, as long as they carry the electronic bug with them, a gang of d4+1 thugs appears every d4+1 days and attempts to waylay the heroes. (Agent Balance doesn't care for loose ends.) It takes that long for each team to acquire the signal in the transmitter range (48 kilometers), which is frighteningly wide for such a small device. The thugs' favorite tactic is ambush from a dark alley, on an abandoned country road, or in a hotel room in the dark of night. Thugs attack until one of them is severely wounded, the attack proceeds for more than

6 rounds, or the sound of distant sirens indicates police are on the way. At this juncture, the thugs do their best to make a clean getaway, utilizing a nearby stolen truck or previously cached car. Of course, heroes may attempt to capture the thugs before they all get away.

Balance anonymously employs many such short-term contract agents. These thugs are usually recruited from extremist hate groups. Depending on their origin, the thugs are told the heroes are IRS agents, leaders of the "crypto-Jewish conspiracy," FBI agents trying to infiltrate the Klan, or left-wing journalists— whatever explanation is likely to incite the goons to violence. In this vein, attacking thugs call out insults and threats such as "Go back to Jerusalem!" or "Leave the Klan alone!"

Hired thugs are ignorant of their employer and receive their pay in unmarked envelopes at the completion of their job. If the heroes have special means to gather information from the thugs, or if they capture one, they discover that at least one thug in every group has a card with the *devermis@yahoo.com* email address, to which periodic progress reports are emailed from public terminals, if possible. If local police become involved in apprehending the thugs, the attack is booked as a simple robbery attempt or possibly a random hate crime (the thugs do nothing to disabuse the police of this notion).

Thugs (d4 + 1)

Level 1 Combat Specs

STR	11	[+1]	INT	9	[0]
DEX	9	[0]	WIL	10	[0]
CON	13		PER	8	

Durability: 13/13/7/7   Action Check: 13+/12/6/3
Move: sprint 20, run 12, walk 4   #Actions: 2
Reaction Score: Ordinary/2   Last Resorts: 0

Attacks

Unarmed	13/7/3	d4s/d4+1s/d4+2s	LI
Knife	13/6/3	d4w/d4+1w/d4+2w	LI/O
Pistol, 9mm	12/6/3	d4w+1/d4+2w/d4m	HI/O

Defenses
+1 resistance modifier vs. melee attacks

Skills
Athletics [11]; Melee [11]–*blade [13];* Unarmed [11]–*brawl [13];* Modern [9]–*pistol [11];* Vehicle Operation [9]; Stamina [13]–*endurance [14];* Knowledge [9]–*language: English [12];* Awareness [10]; Street [10]–*criminal [11];* Interaction [8]–*intimidate [10].*

Gear
9mm pistol, concealed holster, knife, business card containing email address <devermis@yahoo.com>

Scene Two: Charleston, W. Va.

Coordinates:
Lat: 38° 21′ 1″ N
Lon: 81° 37′ 49″ W
Nearest Airport: Yeager Airport
Population: ~58,000
Suggested Lodging: Charleston Marriott Town Center, Lee Street East.

Charleston has amenities of every type, though chain stores and other generic establishments predominate. Other than the forensics lab used by the Charleston police, little else concerning the town is important to the adventure, although the GM can develop this area if desired.

The Charleston police have custody of the body featured in the news clipping and any investigation regarding it. A call to local police (or a local newspaper) rewards heroes with two pieces of information, if they ask the proper questions. First, Detective Sergeant Mark Gordon filed the report concerning the body found along the highway; and second, the Charleston Forensics Lab currently has the body, but no information has yet been released.

Heroes can find Gordon's name and phone number with little difficulty. If they desire, the heroes may merely attempt to interview Gordon over the phone, or they may attempt to arrange a face-to-face interview. Either way, the heroes must convince Gordon to submit to the interview if none of the heroes has affiliations with other law enforcement or security agencies. A reasonable story by the heroes and a successful Interaction–*bluff* or *charm* check convinces Gordon to submit to an interview (each subsequent attempt to interview Gordon suffers a cumulative +1 step penalty).

With the proper questions and successful Interaction–*interview* skill checks, Gordon reveals the following pieces of information and/or takes the mentioned actions:

- The call alerting the police to the body was an anonymous tip, and remains so.
- Gordon was on the scene when the body was retrieved by ambulance, and it was he who filed the police report. The body was found in the westbound lane of I-64 near Exit 28. *Special:* With a successful *interview* check (at a +2 step penalty), Gordon reveals that due to a computer glitch the report has been temporarily lost, although Gordon is confident that it'll all soon be worked out. (He's wrong; Agent Balance has hacked into the police database and erased the file.)
- Gordon called in the Centers for Disease Control because of the questionable condition of the body. The CDC agent who showed up at the scene (in under an hour) was named "Jon Smithy." Of course, if the PCs inquire, no department of the CDC claims to have ever had a Jon Smithy on its payroll. Characters with contacts in the CDC are similarly frustrated in discovering an employee with that name. Furthermore, the CDC never actually received any alert from the police concerning this case (Balance intercepted the cell phone call).

Detective Sergeant Mark Gordon

Police Officer
Level 6 Combat Spec

STR	10	[0]	INT	10	[0]
DEX	11	[+1]	WIL	10	[0]
CON	10		PER	9	

Durability: 10/10/5/5   Action Check: 14+/13/6/3
Move: sprint 20, run 12, walk 4   #Actions: 2
Reaction Score: Ordinary/2   Last Resorts: 1
Perks: Danger Sense [–2 step bonus to *intuition*]
Flaws: Old Injury [bullet wound; suffers 2w and 1s when he jumps or falls more than 1 meter]

Attacks

9mm pistol	13/6/3	d4+1w/d4+2w/d4m	HI/O
Nightstick	11/5/2	d64+1s/d4w/d4+1w	LI/O

Defenses
+1 resistance modifier vs. ranged attacks
Bulletproof vest: d6–3 (LI)/d6–2 (HI)/ d4–2 (En)

Skills
Athletics [10]; Melee [10]–*bludgeon [11]*; Modern [11]–*pistol [12]*; Vehicle [11]–*land [12], air [12]*; Stamina [10]–*endurance [11]*; Knowledge [10]–*computer [11], deduce [11], language: English [13]*; Law [10]–*enforcement [11]*; Security [10]; Awareness–*intuition* [11], perception [12]*; Investigate [10]–*interrogate [11], search [11]*; Resolve [10]; Interaction [9]–*interview [10]*.
    * –2 step bonus

Gear
Police nightstick (club), 9mm pistol, handcuffs, battle vest

Gordon is an honest cop in his mid-40s. His back pains him sometimes from an old bullet wound. He is usually direct and forward in all his statements and interactions.

- The body was strangely bloated, discolored, and leaking a smelly, jellylike fluid—easily the oddest corpse Gordon has ever seen. This anomaly triggered Gordon's CDC alert. Thankfully, Jon Smithy identified the cause of death as severe pneumonia, though to be thorough, Gordon had the body transferred to the Charleston Forensics Lab and into the care of a DR. KLINE.
- Should the heroes convince Detective Sergeant Mark Gordon that something fishy is going on, he offers to join the heroes in their investigation of the forensics lab in an off-duty capacity. The heroes can count on Gordon's assistance while they remain in Charleston. Gordon does not leave the city with the heroes to investigate further, preferring to remain behind to track down the perpetrators of the computer glitch and the reason behind the occurrences at the forensics lab (see below). However,

Gordon could prove to be a party contact in future adventures, if the DM so desires. In the short term, Gordon covers up any "suspicious" evidence the heroes may leave during their excursion to the forensics lab.

Charleston Forensics Lab

The Charleston Forensics Lab is housed separately in a two-story building several blocks from the Charleston police department proper. Heroes who call or stop by with casual questions concerning the lab are treated to a recitation of the lab's virtues (see below). Heroes who specifically ask questions about the bloated female body brought to the lab under Detective Sergeant Gordon's watch are directed to speak to Dr. Kline.

Via the phone or in person (should the heroes visit the lab by without calling first), Dr. Kline speaks only briefly with the heroes. He seems overworked, insisting he can't talk right now. Only if they mention the bloated body found along the road does Dr. Kline switch gears and become more amenable (otherwise the forensics doctor rudely dismisses the heroes). The doctor still claims to be too busy for an immediate interview, but he expresses interest in meeting the PCs and answering their questions in an after-hours face-to-face interview.

With the heroes' approval, he sets up a late meeting at the lab. Kline says he'll let the heroes in after hours at 9:30 P.M., at the rear door next to the loading dock—see room F6. No other arrangement satisfies Dr. Kline—he insists he can only speak at length during the after-hours interview in the forensics building itself. He also claims he has something concerning the body that the heroes might like to see.

Dr. Kline is not an honest man. He uses his position with the police forensics lab to gather biological materials that he offers for resale on the most terrible of black markets. Thus, when a certain Mr. Smithy offered Kline a substantial sum of money to "lose" a particular bloated body and any associated forensic report, the doctor acquiesced. More important, Kline also accepted a hefty bonus to deal with any potential problems or loose ends that might arise in connection with the missing body. The heroes qualify as just such a problem. Kline's invitation to talk after hours is part of a trap the good doctor arranges in order to put an end to the heroes' investigation.

Forensics Lab, Keyed Entries

Refer to "Charleston Forensics Lab" in the interior front cover map for the locations of the following keyed entries.

By day, the two-story building presents an average-looking exterior, although the first floor has only a single window. Should the heroes arrive by night, the building takes on an altogether more sinister profile in the weak street lamps.

Unknown to Kline, Balance sends some extra muscle (one AHD handler) to ensure that Kline deals with any problems that arise. Dr. Kline sets up his own ambush for the PCs, and the handler (having overheard the doctor's plan) waits to see how it plays out before involving himself. (See the particulars noted in room F6.) The agent is fully aware of the importance of disposing potential investigators in a clean, nonnewsworthy manner.

F1. Lobby
By day, the main entrance to the building is unlocked.

The room is somewhat harshly lit by rows of ceiling fluorescent tubes, which reveal a several faux leather seats, stands littered with out-of-date magazines, and a wide desk complete with a grape-colored iMac.

The receptionist is Todd Brown. (Todd is a temp, and he spends most days reading philosophy textbooks—use the Marginal Administrator statistics in the *Gamemaster Guide,* if necessary.) The receptionist answers general questions (see "About the Forensics Lab," above), but he refers all specific questions to the head doctor, Dr. Kline. See above for Kline's actions and agenda.

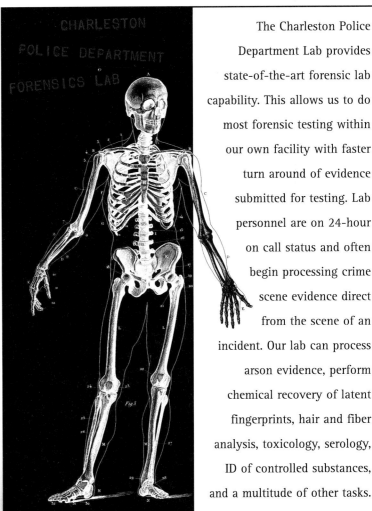

The Charleston Police Department Lab provides state-of-the-art forensic lab capability. This allows us to do most forensic testing within our own facility with faster turn around of evidence submitted for testing. Lab personnel are on 24-hour on call status and often begin processing crime scene evidence direct from the scene of an incident. Our lab can process arson evidence, perform chemical recovery of latent fingerprints, hair and fiber analysis, toxicology, serology, ID of controlled substances, and a multitude of other tasks.

By night, the main entrance is locked, and only a single row of fluorescent lights illuminates the room. Usually, a night guard is posted here reading magazines (Alfred Turing, a 1st-level Combat Spec—use Ordinary Brawler statistics, if necessary), but on the night the heroes make an appointment to meet Dr. Kline, the doctor arranges to allow Turing a night off, conveniently forgetting to requisition a replacement.

F2. Stairs
These stairs connect the first and second floors.

F3. Stairs
These stairs connect the first floor and the basement.

F4. Forensic Labs
Three labs are keyed to this entry.

The forensics lab contains four steel examining tables, each situated directly under a high-wattage lamp array. The floors are tiled, except for the conspicuous drains. Industrial-sized sinks compete for counter space with microscopes, scales, and other analytical equipment along the walls. Shelves and racks above the counters contain all manner of medical equipment useful for both fine and gross "inquiries."

By day, d4 forensic doctors labor here over bodies whose manner of passing is in question. The doctors are randomly selected from the names given in the description of room F10.

By night, the doors to these labs are locked, and all is generally quiet. Unknown to Dr. Kline, however, an AHD handler sent by Balance waits here to ensure that the company's classified work remains secret. The handler's name is Jim Williams.

Searches through these labs do not reveal anything likely to excite a conspiracy-minded character. However, potentially useful items may be salvaged here, including formaldehyde and other chemicals, syringes with needles, and scalpels of all sizes.

F5. Body Bank
The freezerlike door to this chamber is locked, day or night. The lock is on the outside.

The chilly chamber is walled on all sides by banks of metallic 50-cm-by-50-cm metal drawers, three drawers high. Several height-adjustable metal carts stand in the chamber's center.

A small plaque on the front of each drawer contains a file number ten digits long, corresponding to one of the case files for various autopsies stored on computers in the offices keyed to F10. Each drawer pulls open easily and is 50% likely to contain a body under a sheet. Though a wide range of reasons for death is apparent from study of these chilled forms, none of them appears to have died by any unusual means.

F6. Ready Room
The exterior door is usually locked, but the two interior doors are not. If the heroes have an after-hours appointment with Dr. Kline, the exterior door is unlocked at 9:00 P.M.

Jim Williams

AHD Security Specialist (handler)
Level 6 Combat Spec

STR	10	[0]		INT	10	[0]
DEX	11	[+1]		WIL	10	[0]
CON	10			PER	9	

Durability: 10/10/5/5   Action Check: 14+/13/6/3
Move: sprint 20, run 12, walk 4   #Actions: 2
Reaction Score: Ordinary/2   Last Resorts: 1

Attacks
9mm pistol	13/6/3	d4+1w/d4+2w/d4m	HI/O
Unarmed	11/5/2	d6s/d6+2s/d4w	LI/O

Defenses
+1 resistance modifier vs. ranged attacks
Battle vest: d6–3 (LI)/d6–2 (HI)/ d4–2 (En)

Skills
Athletics [10]; Unarmed [10]–*power [11]*; Modern [11]–*pistol [13]*; Stealth [11]–*shadow [12], sneak [12]*; Vehicle Operation [11]; Stamina [10]–*endurance [11]*; Knowledge [10]–*computer [11], deduce [11], language: English [13]*; Law [10]; Security [10]–*protocols [11], devices [12]*; System Operation [10]; Awareness [10]–*intuition [11], perception [12]*; Investigate [10]–*interrogate [11]*; Resolve [10]–*mental [11]*; Interaction [9]–*intimidate [11]*.

Gear
Bulletproof vest, 9mm pistol and ammo, shoulder holster, miniature radio with earpiece (1.5 kilometer range), sunglasses (tint varies with light conditions), stimulants, expensive Timex watch (electronically bugged)

Boxes of all sizes are neatly stacked along the south wall, and large metal cabinets line the shorter north wall. The west wall holds metal shelving upon which 2-liter amber jugs are stacked in neat lines. Large metal drums stand upright in the room's center, two deep in a row running east–west. The smell of organic solvents is thick in spite of the constant thrum of heavy-duty ventilation fans mounted in ceiling ducts.

Heroes keeping an appointment at 9:30 find Dr. Kline in this chamber. (If they arrive early, they find a polite note asking them to please wait, because the doctor is engaged in finishing a report.) Otherwise, the room generally remains unoccupied. The ready room is filled with all manner of supplies and chemicals common to a medical facility, including several grades of sulfuric acid and acetic acid in handy 2-liter glass bottles. (All of these acids may be treated as the acids described in the *Gamemaster Guide;* see Table G14.) Some of the large barrels are filled with pure ethanol, while others serve as receptacles for organic waste. Two gas masks lie on top of one of the

Dr. Julius Kline

Forensics Doctor
Level 6 Tech Op

STR	8	[0]		INT	12	[+1]
DEX	11	[+1]		WIL	12	[+1]
CON	10			PER	7	

Durability: 10/10/5/5
Move: sprint 18, run 12, walk 4
Reaction Score: Ordinary/2
Achievements: Action Check Bonus [–1 step bonus to action checks]

Action Check: 13+/12/6/3
#Actions: 2
Last Resorts: 0

Attacks

Syringe*	9/4/2	d4-2s/d4-1s/d4s	LI/O
Unarmed**	4/2/1	d4s/d4+1s/d4+2s	LI/O

*Anesthetic: If 1 point of primary damage gets past a hero's armor, the paralytic poison takes effect. Insinuative (injected): CON feat check at a +3 step penalty to resist. Failure = knocked out; Ordinary success = +3 step penalty to all actions; Good success = +2 step penalty; Amazing success = +1 step penalty. Onset time 1 round, duration 30 minutes. Six anesthetic doses per syringe.

**+d4 base situation die.

Defenses

+1 resistance modifier vs. ranged attacks
+1 INT resistance vs. encounter checks
+1 WIL resistance vs. encounter checks
Lab coat, leaded   d6–4 (LI)/d6–3 (HI)/d4–1 (En)

Skills

Athletics [8]; Melee [8]–blade [9]; Vehicle [11]–land [13]; Stamina [10]; Knowledge [12]–computer [13], deduce [13], language: English [15]; Life [12]–biology [13]; Medical [12]–forensics [13], knowledge [13]; Physical [12]–chemistry [13]; Business [12]–illicit [13]; Awareness [12]–intuition [13], perception [13]; Lore [12]–fringe [13]; Resolve [12]; Interaction [7].

Gear

Lead-lined lab coat, syringe of anesthetic, keys to all rooms in building

waste barrels. Prolonged exposure to the fumes in this chamber (10 minutes) requires a Stamina–endurance check. Anyone failing the check (except for the janitor Melvin Harms—see below) suffers a +1 step penalty for all actions until he or she can breathe clean air for 10 minutes. The exposure time/debilitating effects are cumulative.

The good doctor arrives in the ready room to meet the heroes at the appointed time. Otherwise, he works in his office (F11) all day and late into the night. Dr. Kline is in his late 50s, with a handsome well-groomed silvery hair and beard, and he wears a lab coat over shirt and slacks. If more than three PCs arrive, Kline seems surprised and momentarily uneasy at the appearance of so many investigators.

Kline waves away initial questions, saying only, "We'll talk after I show you something, something incredible. This way." Kline motions for his guests to follow him into the hallway connecting F7 and F8. If Kline cannot convince the heroes to enter the hallway or if the situation otherwise changes, Melvin abandons his ambush post and enters the room at the end of the following round to aid Dr. Kline.

Kline's Ambush:

- If the good doctor persuades the heroes out of room F6 and into the dimly lit hallway between F7 and F8, he resolutely takes the lead, heading toward the elevator (F8).
- The ambush is set to occur when Kline and the heroes are halfway down the hallway. At this time, the door into the hallway from F7 opens, and a large man in a blue janitor's uniform emerges, pushing a garbage cart. This is Melvin Harms (see F7). As preorchestrated, Kline pauses, and Melvin calls out in a vaguely grotesque mumble, "Dr. Kline, hold the elevator, please." Melvin uses this time to close the distance between himself and the hero at the end of the procession.
- Unless the heroes have previously alerted the GM that they are on their guard, they are taken by surprise (the attackers gain an

Melvin Harms

Brawler
Level 3 Combat Spec

STR	11	[+1]	INT	7	[0]
DEX	10	[0]	WIL	11	[+1]
CON	14		PER	7	

Durability: 14/14/7/7   Action Check: 12+/11/5/2
Move: sprint 14, run 10, walk 4   #Actions: 3
Reaction Score: Ordinary/2   Last Resorts: 0
Perk: Tough as Nails (applied)

Attacks

Shears	14/7/3	d4+2w/d4+3w/d4+4w	LI/O
Unarmed	14/7/3	d4+2s/d4+3s/d4+4s	LI/O

Defenses

+2 resistance modifier vs. melee attacks (includes perk)
+1 WIL resistance modifier vs. encounter checks

Skills

Athletics [11]–*climb [13], jump [12]*; Melee [11]–*blade [14]*; Unarmed [11]–*brawl [14]*; Stealth [10]; Vehicle Operation [10]; Stamina [14]–*endurance [15], resist pain [15]*; Knowledge [7]–*language: English [10]*; Awareness [11]–*perception [12]*; Interaction [7]–*intimidate [9], taunt [8]*.

Gear

Shears, janitor's gear, souvenir knucklebone, keys to all rooms in building except Kline's office

---

extra phase of action before the round begins) when Melvin grabs up rusty gardening shears secreted in his cart and viciously attacks the nearest hero. Simultaneously, Kline pulls out a syringe filled with anesthetic and from his position at the front of the procession attempts to waylay the nearest hero (see Kline's statistics for information on the anesthetic).

- The AHD agent waits until the ambush has begun and watches carefully from his position at F4. He's been watching Kline and the heroes to make sure Kline really does tries to take care of them on his own. If it becomes obvious that Kline will fail, the agent begins shooting down the hall, trying to pick off the PCs one by one.

Kline hopes to anesthetize or otherwise kill off the heroes, and, if successful, he plans on storing anesthetized investigators in the body bank (F5) and incinerating dead heroes (F13). On the other hand, if the heroes appear to be winning, Kline attempts to flee under the cover of Harms's and the handler's covering fire, so that he can hide in another part of the building. In fact, the GM should attempt to create a cat-and-mouse chase through the whole dark forensics lab. If Kline fails to escape and is caught, heroes may at-

tempt to pump him for information. If they kill the doctor or otherwise fail to get information out him, the investigators have the recourse of locating and searching Kline's office (F11) for clues.

The doctor was paid by a mysterious Mr. Smithy to get rid of the bloated body and delete all forensic records of it. A record of the doctor's illicit activities exists in files on his office computer and in his physical file cabinets (see F11). The doctor reveals this only under intense questioning, but does not give up anything directly. A search through Kline's wallet reveals a <devermis@yahoo.com> business card, but Kline isn't talking. The words "Specimen X" have been written on the back of the card, indicating the file name (both physical and computer) where the information regarding Kline's dealings with the body is recorded.

F7. Loading Dock

The interior doors are usually unlocked, but the large loading door remains locked unless a delivery is in progress.

The sliding garage door of the loading dock takes up most of the east wall. Several empty metal hospital gurneys are stacked on shelves along the south wall, amid a variety of other clutter. A janitor's station graces the north wall.

Melvin Harms, the facility janitor, claims this station. Melvin can normally be found puttering about this chamber for 30 minutes out of every hour (the remainder of each hour he spends cleaning the rest of the building). However, on any night when Kline sets up for "special" projects, Melvin lurks here to give the doc a hand. On the night the heroes have their appointment with Kline, Melvin waits here for the prearranged ambush cue (see F6).

This large area serves as a dropoff and pickup point for cadavers brought to and taken from the Charleston Forensics Lab. Aside from the gurneys and a variety of janitorial supplies, nothing of importance stands out here.

F8. Elevator

This elevator connects all three floors of the facility: basement, first floor, and second floor.

F9. Landing

A couple of large tables and chairs, a coffee machine, and a water cooler transform this wide landing into an open conference area.

F10. Offices

During the weekday, these offices are usually in use by the associate doctors of the facility. At night, the doors are normally locked. The large offices are similar, the only significant differences being in decor. The name of each associate doctor is stenciled upon the door: 1) Richard Edberg, 2) Michael Hodge, 3) Sharon Gianopoulos, 4) Robert Butler, 5) Andrea Zimmerman, 6) Paul Carrol, 7) Steve Kron, and 8) Daniel Talcot.

A Power Macintosh G3 competes for desk space with loose files, books, coffee mugs, and miscellaneous office supplies. Drab filing cabinets and shelves filled with medical texts, reference material, and small knickknacks round out the office.

Files on the associate doctors' computers link many of the file numbers on the drawers in the body bank (F5) with names; however, no evidence of the bloated body, or J. S. (Jane Scarborough), is recorded on any computer or the server database.

F11. Dr. Kline's Office

Like the other offices, the door contains a stenciled name: Dr. Julius Kline, Director. The door is always locked, even if Kline is inside. If the investigators have made it this far without running into or speaking with Dr. Kline previously, the good doctor indicates he

devermis@yahoo.com

This is one of many email accounts owned by AHD agent Andrew Balance. He has a few business cards containing only this information, which he leaves for those with whom he wishes to maintain contact. Those who email the devermis account soon receive an email response: Subject: Yahoo! Mail Auto-Reply, "Be patient. Your message is being routed to my exact location. When I have read your message, I will find you. Wait right there," from JON SMITHY (Smithy is an alias, of course). Agent Balance, as a general rule, makes certain to keep his contacts (of all types) with the heroes as mysterious as possible, as long as possible, in order to engender paranoia and outright fear. **GM Note:** If the players have email access, encourage them to try this address out for themselves!

Furthermore, Balance traces those who email him with his uplinked laptop computer. Within 1d4 hours of receiving any message at <devermis@yahoo.com>, Balance makes a Computer Science–*hacking* skill check (see Balance's statistics under "Wrap-up: Act One, Scene Three"). Any success allows Balance to trace an unsecured email account, discovering any information recorded in the PC's email account (if the PC's real name is recorded on the email account, Balance learns it, plus geographical data and interests). An Amazing result allows Balance to trace a dummy email account up the chain to the next email account, if any. Each time a hero emails "Smithy," Balance attempts to trace the chain of dummy accounts (if any), up one level per attempt, until the hero's real name is discovered. Heroes remain unaware of this activity unless they make an Awareness–*intuition* check at a +2 step penalty, followed by a Computer Science–*hacking* check. These checks alone are not enough to forestall Balance, but they do alert the heroes to "Smithy's" activities.

Should Balance trace heroes he hasn't already identified through the course of the adventure, he enters their names and likenesses into the AHD database, making it more difficult for the investigators to openly enter any AHD facility. He also sends email to the hero's top-level account, if any, identifying the hero by name and conveying the message "Now that I know who you are, your time on earth grows short." Balance hopes to create a sense of paranoia in those who would trifle with him and his agenda.

would be more than happy to talk, but at a later appointed time—see "Contacting Doctor Kline" above.

At first glance, Dr. Kline's office is much like the others (F10), though larger and with more filing cabinets. A search through the filing cabinets or computer files aids the PCs in their investigation. Heroes who already know what file to look for (Specimen X) find both a computer file and a hard-copy duplicate with little trouble. Those who are looking for interesting files without foreknowledge must make a successful Investigate–*search* or *research* check to find the correct file.

Kline's Specimen X File: The file consists of five MS Word documents labeled "Contract," "Addendum," "Disposition," "Speculation," and "Anomaly." The documents' dates indicate that they were written in the order presented, each a day or two after the previous one. If the heroes moved fast enough so that Kline had less time with the body, compress the time scale; he performed an immediately analysis, intrigued by its condition and Balance's threat.

Contract: "Smithy says he'll pay well for my services. I don't think that's his real name, and I don't trust him, but what choice do I have? Says he'll blow the whistle on my little 'side business' if I don't accept his contract. Well, damn it, I'll take his money and I'll make J.S., whatever her real name was, disappear. It'll be as if the cadaver never existed. Still, there is something very strange about it. It probably wouldn't hurt to save an autopsy sample for myself. I wonder what the real cause of death was."

Addendum: "Mysterious Mr. Smithy is getting on my nerves. Now I have to 'deal' with anyone who shows up asking about the body. Well, I'll take care of any snoopers permanently; it's not like I haven't taken similar steps when my black-market body-parts venture was almost discovered. Mr. Harms is dumb as a post, but will prove useful in this task nonetheless."

Disposition: "REMEMBER to DELETE this file. Anterior sample remnant: hidden in basement in an old Ethanol drum in the northeast corner chalked with initials "J.S." Personal effects: Effects Repository, Locker 23. Must remove sample and effects from lab as soon as possible."

Speculation: "This is remarkable—the woman died from some sort of total-body transformation, effected at a genetic level. Possibly the result of covert gene therapy? Damn, I'm shaking . . . it looks like she died from a massive dose of collagenase, secreted from her own skin cells! The collagenase liquefied her internal organs, producing a body cavity of gangrenous gel. I can't understand how the epidermal skin layer remained active and vital, while at the same time the interior was necrotized. It almost looks like body was transforming into a jellyfish. I've identified several too-large microorganisms (macroorganisms?) still active in the epidermal layer. Under the microscope, the organisms continually exude countless tiny fingerlike projections, like tentacles. The projections appear, change shape, and disappear on a time scale of minutes! I hope they're not infectious."

Anomaly: "I sent a sample vial of the little buggers out to one of my fringe 'business contacts.' Fellow called back, saying he'd give me ten times the normal bonus for the whole biosample—he was pretty excited. Asked what was so important about it. He claimed the sample contained TPA. What the heck is that? He muttered something about 'genetic material . . . not DNA.' How can that be? He won't even tell me what TPA stands for, but if he pays me what I'm asking, I'll give him the sample."

GM Note: The specifics of Dr. Kline's body-part business and the potential buyer noted above is not important to the adventure as written and is not developed as an encounter, though additional complications are possible at the GM's option.

F12. Effects Repository

Steel metal lockers line the walls of this chamber, and a double row of lockers forms an island in the room's center. The lockers are numbered.

The door to the repository is normally locked, requiring a successful Manipulation–*lockpick* skill check to open. Sometimes the possessions of those to be autopsied accompany the bodies. Prior to being remanded to family members or to police as evidence, such effects are stored here. A general search through all the lockers reveals a smattering of wallets, purses, and related belongings. Heroes indifferent to ethical concerns may be tempted to loot each wallet and purse—a total of $796.47 can be gathered in this ignominious fashion.

Locker 23 contains a glossy flier, a filthy lab coat, a muddy and torn composition book, and a handkerchief with the initials "J.S." on it.

The composition book contains the sentence "This record is the truth" on the inside leaf. Jane intended to write a revealing essay in the composition book, but was laid low by the *C. cnidarae* infection before she had the opportunity. The first page of the composition book is torn out, and does not accompany the book.

GM Note: It's only because of Agent Balance's appearance on the scene that this booklet was not found by the police. The heroes should eventually find the torn-out page inside the burial mound of Chief Cornstalk. See Scene Three of this act, area B4.

The glossy flier discusses a festival set to occur in the very near future. (The GM should determine the exact dates, in order to coincide with heroes' potential arrival in Point Pleasant.) The flier contains a few scenes of a festival in a small town, with the accompanying text:

The annual Point Pleasant Sternwheel Regatta! Come see flat-bottomed steamers race on the Ohio River! Come see fireworks displays and live entertainment! Come see West Virginia's ONLY Antique Bottle Show! To be held at the American Legion Hall, corner of Twenty-third and Main streets, Thursday, Friday, Saturday, and Sunday, from 10 A.M.–10 P.M. Features all types of bottles, antique and historic, dealers from all over the region, and much more, including historic collectibles.

In addition to the printed text, the flier has two handwritten sentences scrawled on it:

Dr. Shabbir confirms Cornstalk connection.

The talisman is my only hope.

The flier is a souvenir Jane grabbed during her desperate visit to Point Pleasant. This flier points the heroes directly at Scene Three of this act. The scrawled handwriting on the flier is Jane Scarborough's, matching the handwriting in the composition book. It also provides a Point Pleasant contact (Dr. Shabbir).

The filthy, ragged lab coat bears no distinguishing marks; however, a small Sharp scientific calculator rests in the left-hand pocket. The calculator still works, but switching it on also secretly activates another electronic bug cleverly embedded in the calculator. Taking the calculator with them means the heroes are bugged (this replaces the bug on the original purse if the heroes found it). Discovering this bug is only possible if the calculator is opened up and a Security–*security devices* or Technical Science skill check is successful. Bugged heroes are in the situation described in Act One, Scene One.

F13. Basement

The basement is a wide, damp space enclosed by unfinished cement. A few bare bulbs provide inadequate light. Besides fuse boxes, wiring, plumbing, and the bare ductwork associated with most basements, several dozen empty metallic drums clutter the side walls. A very large incinerator/heater squats against the center of the east wall, vintage early 1900s. As you peer into the darkened room, you are startled by a sudden metallic "thump."

Foreknowledge or a thorough search of every drum discovers one barrel still sealed with a lid and a padlock, requiring a Manipulation–*lockpick* skill check. The barrel is lightly chalked with the initials J.S. This barrel contains Kline's "anterior sample." In fact, Dr. Kline removed the head from Jane Scarborough's body, placed it in a Hefty garbage bag, and put the bag in the barrel. Kline burned the rest of the cadaver in the nearby incinerator.

As Kline noted in his computer files, the tissue retained bioactivity. Though Jane Scarborough is long dead, the macroorganisms responsible for her demise continued to alter the necrotic flesh to suit—it has become a creature unto itself. Safe from tampering in the barrel, the disembodied head is now com-

pletely transparent and hairless, though "head" is too generous a term—it has become a tertiary cnidocyte. Six slender, translucent tentacles have sprouted from the cnidocyte in a radially symmetrical pattern, though the vacant expression on the original translucent shape remains horribly distinct (the residual shape usually lasts d12 days, before slumping). The tentacles grant the thing limited movement and also have stinging NEMATOCYSTS. If the heroes open the drum and peer in, the cnidocyte dramatically extrudes its tentacles and attacks! Unless the players have alerted the GM that the heroes are on their guard, they are taken by surprise (the attackers gain an extra phase of action before the round begins) when the attack occurs.

See Act One, Scene One for tertiary cnidocyte statistics and details.

F14. Restrooms

Men's and women's restrooms, kept clean and sanitary by the friendly Mr. Harms.

Wrap-up: Act One, Scene Two

If all goes well, the heroes make a definitive connection between the car thief and Jane Scarborough. Moreover, they have direct evidence linking Scarborough's recent visit to Point Pleasant and a certain Dr. Shabbir. If the heroes decide to check out Point Pleasant, Dr. Shabbir, and the Sternwheel Regatta, refer to Scene Three of this act.

If the heroes do not burn the body of the tertiary cnidocyte encountered in the basement of the Charleston Forensics Lab (or otherwise sterilize the tissue by dousing it in acetic acid or dunking it in formaldehyde), it recovers full health in 10 days. Heroes who have left the creature behind need not concern themselves with this, but those who take the body with them are in for a rude surprise. Should the heroes attempt to show their specimen to authorities or medical specialists, the smelly, slimy corpse is identified as a jellyfish (the similarity to the late Jane Scarborough's features has faded by now). Even heroes determined to make a revelation with their prize are frustrated by most people's intractable desire to remain firmly in the bounds of the reasonable. Only the reanimation of the "jellyfish" at precisely the wrong moment might cause a specialist to change his mind, and the GM should avoid this occurrence unless it in some way advances the plot, not endangers it.

At some point the heroes may decide that, while interesting, the ultimate fate of Jane Scarborough doesn't warrant further investigation, especially if none of the heroes succumbs to *C. cnidarae*. Getting the heroes back on track might require a contact from the Hoffmann Institute or a similarly helpful group. The contact comes in the form of a simple envelope delivered to the heroes at their hotel or residence. Inside, a piece of paper reads: "A bonus [type or amount determined by GM] is available to any investigative team that can confirm or allay the Institute's fears concerning reports of secret biological weapons development. Though it is only a slim lead, the Institute has discovered that the supposed CDC agent at the scene of the murder of an unidentified woman last Friday was a fake—the CDC was not involved, though it obviously should have been. We suspect coverup, but from whom? Follow all

available leads; get to the bottom of this." The letter may be unsigned, or signed with the name of a contact claimed by one of the heroes.

Additionally, heroes who have remained in the area catch a news report carried by the local media: Lester Mason, a tow lot operator, has been killed by a single bullet to the back of the head. Police are requesting anyone with information about the crime to step forward. Agent Balance is cleaning up loose ends; paranoid heroes may realize that it's only a matter of time before he catches up with them.

Scene Three: Point Pleasant, W. Va.

Coordinates:
  Lat: 38° 51' 13" N
  Lon: 82° 7' 50" W
Nearest Airport: Mason County Airport
Population: ~5,000
Suggested Lodging: Stone Manor Bed & Breakfast, Main St., Point Pleasant WV 25550.

Point Pleasant is a small town with a long history. Although chain stores and other generic establishments can be found, "Mom & Pop" establishments of various types still thrive here, as well as many stores that specialize in homemade crafts.

Heroes who call ahead or do Internet and/or conventional research easily discover two points of information. First, Dr. Shabbir (a chiropractor) has an office in Point Pleasant, though no residential listing is available. However, a recorded message indicates Dr. Shabbir's office is closed for a month, partly due to a personal vacation and partly due to the Sternwheel Regatta (he has a booth in the antique bottles show). Second, the Sternwheel Regatta is a four-day-long festival that features flat-bottomed steamer races on the nearby Ohio River (which borders the state of Ohio), and also includes many other family activities and entertainment.

Characters versed in paranormal lore may also recognize Point Pleasant as the location of the famous "mothman sightings" of the 1960s. The Lexicon in the Introduction includes information such heroes may already know or can easily discover.

The Regatta

The festival draws people from all over Mason County, and Point Pleasant's population grows from 5,000 to nearly 20,000 during the height of the celebration. Commercial streets swell with people all day and far into the night. Pavilions, booths, and small tents temporarily form secondary street fronts and spill into parks like multicolored shanty towns. Antiques, crafts, specialty foods, entertainment, and more can be had at the Sternwheel Regatta.

If the heroes visit Point Pleasant while the regatta is in full swing, a lot is going on. Without much effort at all, the heroes can acquire

Sternwheel Regatta Schedule

Thursday
Antique Bottle Display Opens....................9 a.m.–3 p.m.
Queen Pageant...10 a.m.
Fireworks..7 p.m.

Friday
Antique Bottle Display...............................9 a.m.–3 p.m.
3-On-3 Basketball Tourney Semifinals...11 a.m.
Parade...4 p.m.
Bellamy Brothers Main Stage....................7 p.m.
Fireworks..9 p.m.

Saturday
Antique Bottle Display...............................9 a.m.–3 p.m.
5K River Run...10 a.m.
3-On-3 Basketball Tourney Final..............11 a.m.
Sternwheeler Races..12 p.m.
Saturday Night Showcases.........................6 p.m.
    Featuring Mick Souter, Zydeco Bon,
    Standish Drive & the Photons

Sunday
Antique Bottle Display...............................9 a.m.–3 p.m.
"Anything That Floats" Race.....................10 a.m.
Soccer Tournament.......................................12 p.m.
Fireworks Grand Finale...............................7 p.m.

type are presented for perusal and display, and a few booths offer an assortment of other antique items. Asking around, or a few minutes of searching, is sufficient to point the heroes toward Dr. Shabbir's booth.

One booth has several glass display cases predominantly filled with arrowheads, above which a banner proudly proclaims "Indian Artifacts, the Vernon Shabbir Collection." Dr. Shabbir can be found here, enthusiastically explaining to all and sundry the wonders of arrowheads, tomahawks, axes, beadwork, baskets, and other historic and prehistoric artifacts of the region.

Whether the heroes contact Dr. Shabbir at his booth, by phone, or through some other means, the artifact enthusiast reacts the same way as soon as they ask him any question about mothmen, Jane Scarborough, Cornstalk, or the "talisman"—he becomes flustered, scared, and cautious. He clams up, insisting he doesn't know what the heroes could possibly be talking about.

If roleplaying cues are not sufficient to convince the heroes that Dr. Shabbir knows more than he lets on, a simple Awareness–*perception* or *intuition* skill check reveals the same. Luckily, Dr. Shabbir is inclined more toward trust than paranoia, and heroes with even a modicum of tact can convince Shabbir that they are merely investigators and do not seek to harm anyone. A successful encounter skill check also convinces Shabbir to open up.

Alternative: If the heroes choose not to speak directly to Shabbir, the information noted below remains important for the heroes to obtain. At the GM's discretion, this information is also all available in Shabbir's diary, which he keeps in a briefcase. The briefcase can be found behind his booth in the American Legion Hall during the Regatta. The heroes must learn about the connection between the Point Pleasant mothman, Chief Cornstalk, the talisman, and Chief Cornstalk's secret burial mound (in the form of the "TNT" area map). Most important, they need Shabbir's hand-drawn diagram of a filled-in circle surrounded by seven additional concentric circles, above which several stars are drawn (the symbol is the key to gaining entry, as described in B1 below).

If the heroes gain Shabbir's trust, he says he'll answer what questions he can, but the interview must be at a location of his choosing. Shabbir selects the very public Morrow's Deli on nearby Jackson Street for the interview. At the time of the appointment (which could be almost immediately after Dr. Shabbir agrees to talk), the heroes find Dr. Shabbir ensconced at a table at the small establishment. Over lunch or dinner, and with successful Interaction–*interview* skill checks, Dr. Shabbir reveals the following pieces of information:

- "J.S.? I don't . . . oh, do you mean Jane Scarborough? She contacted me a while back, asking all sorts of questions about my specialty. I'm an amateur local historian and Indian artifact col-

a schedule of events. They may even want to relax and enjoy the festive atmosphere. If the heroes spend time looking for Dr. Shabbir and acting on the information he provides, the schedule of events allows the GM to interweave an interesting counterpoint to the heroes' grim discoveries and nighttime explorations.

Dr. Shabbir

As indicated in a prerecorded phone message, and as confirmed by a laminated notice on the door to Dr. Shabbir's office (a phone book or the Internet provides the office address at 2124 Jefferson Blvd., Point Pleasant WV 25550), the chiropractor's office is currently closed. However, both the phone message and the sign indicate that Dr. Shabbir can be found during festival hours at the American Legion Hall (corner of 23rd and Main), where Shabbir has a booth.

The convention space within the hall hosts an antique bottle show (plus other antiques and collectibles) during the Sternwheel Regatta. Booths run up and down the floor in typical convention style. At any given time, two hundred to four hundred people mill through the overheated area. Antique bottles of every imaginable

Dr. Vernon Shabbir

Chiropractor (historian)
Level 5 Tech Op

STR	10	[0]	INT	13	[+2]
DEX	9	[0]	WIL	11	[+1]
CON	10		PER	7	

Durability: 10/10/5/6
Move: sprint 18, run 12, walk 4
Reaction Score: Ordinary/2
Perks: Good Luck

Action Check: 13+/12/6/3
#Actions: 2
Last Resorts: 0

Attacks
Unarmed*　　5/2/1　　d4s/d4+1s/d4+2s
　　* +d4 base situation die.

Defenses
+2 INT modifier vs. encounter checks
+1 WIL modifier vs. encounter checks

Skills
Athletics [10]; Vehicle Operation [9]; Stamina [10]; Knowledge [13]–*deduce [15], language: English [16], language: Shawnee [14]*; Social [13]–*anthropology [15], history [15]*; Life [13]–*biology [14], xenology [14]*; Medical [13]–*knowledge [15], treatment [15]*; Awareness [11]–*intuition [13], perception [12]*; Investigate [11]–*research [12], search [12]*; Lore [11]–*occult [13], UFO [12]*; Resolve [11]–*mental [12]*; Interaction [7].

Gear
Several loose arrowheads in pockets, briefcase filled with notes about mothmen, Chief Cornstalk, and the incantation necessary to enter Cornstalk's burial mound

lector. She never told me where she came from or why she was so desperate to learn what I know."

- "What did Scarborough want to know? Well, you may not know it, but Point Pleasant is famous in certain circles for mothman sightings that occurred here back in '67. Anyway, I'm one of those folks who know mothmen really appeared here. I've got proof. Somehow, Jane found out about me, and my theory about mothmen and Chief Cornstalk, who died two hundred years ago. That's what she wanted to know about."

- "The Point Pleasant mothman is often described as a man-sized winged creature shrouded in darkness, except for two glowing red eyes that give viewers the willies. Unbelievers think it's a sandhill crane, a very large bird with red patches around its eyes. After all, the MCCLINTIC WILDLIFE MANAGEMENT AREA is nearby. Anyway, I know different, mostly because I've seen mothmen (there are more than one!) myself."

- "The mothmen I've seen are bipedal but larger than man-size, with a pair of small forelimbs, powerful sweeping wings, and strangely jointed legs that end in clawed feet. They always have two wide red eyes—glowing eyes you can never forget, especially in dreams."

- "My interest in mothmen stems from my interest in the history of the region. See, the Shawnee lived hereabouts before white settlers pushed them out. Their last leader, Chief Cornstalk, was murdered by disgruntled soldiers, but with his dying breath Cornstalk pronounced a curse on the area, which summoned the mothman. Anyway, my own research indicates that this 'curse' wasn't so much a request for vengeance as an appeal for help. Using an ancient talisman, Chief Cornstalk called the mothman, which guards his burial mound to this day!"

- "My research indicates that Chief Cornstalk was a shaman adept whose lore descended from the archaic peoples who first settled this part of North America over fifteen thousand years ago. Apparently, he possessed some sort of talisman that gave him the ability to call forth specific creatures from the spirit world into the world of flesh. By all accounts, this is the talisman Cornstalk used to call the mothman. The talisman is buried with the chief."

- "Chief Cornstalk's burial mound is located near the TNT area north of town, but this isn't information you'll find in any history book. I've been to the mound, and I know how to get in. I told Jane Scarborough the location of the burial mound, because she seemed so desperate."

- "During World War the TNT area was used by a handful of companies to manufacture explosives contracted by the government. Facilities, power plants, ponds, and nearly one hundred igloos were constructed in the area. The igloos were used to store explosives and were covered with dirt, so they couldn't be seen from the air. Most of the igloos are still there today. Funny thing is, a covered igloo looks a lot like Chief Cornstalk's burial mound—coincidence is odd that way."

- "A . . . what? Ambulatory jellyfish? Never heard of anything like that. Sounds disgusting."

- "No, I never met Jane face to face; we talked over the phone and the Internet, and I faxed her a map of the TNT area and burial mound. She did sound under the weather the last time we spoke, but I assumed she had the flu."

- "I don't know where Jane worked, but a couple of times she said, 'I think they're after me.' She never explained who 'they' were, though. Jane and I made an appointment to head out to the burial mound under cover of night, but she never showed up, and I haven't heard from her since. That's strange, because she said something about the talisman being her 'one hope,' whatever that means." **GM Note:** Jane's *C. cnidarae* infection affected her mind, and in her befuddled state she attempted to enter the mound by herself, before a frightening encounter and her deteriorating mental state caused her to drive away from her one possibility of salvation. Later, even more befuddled, she left the stolen car along the side of the road and wandered along the highway before finally collapsing, dead of her infection.

- If the heroes express interest in seeing the mound, or if they tell Shabbir about their own investigation and Jane's ultimate fate, Shabbir offers to guide the heroes to the mound and provide access onsite. If some misadventure makes it impossible for Shabbir to enter the mound with the heroes, he reveals the mound's location and the diagram necessary to enter it. If the heroes allow it, Dr. Shabbir accompanies the PCs throughout the rest of this adventure, as he is fascinated by mothmen and their connection to ancient cultures. He's never been inside the mound himself, mostly due to nervousness, but he's more than willing to go with the PCs.

At the conclusion of the heroes' talk with Dr. Shabbir, they should realize that the only way their investigation can continue is by visiting Chief Cornstalk's secret grave. See the next section, "TNT Area & Burial Mound."

TNT Area & Burial Mound

Either through talking with Shabbir or finding his notes, the heroes learn the information they require to locate the secret burial mound of Chief Cornstalk near the TNT area. See the TNT Area map on the interior front cover. (Shabbir actually has a map very similar to the TNT Area map, which heroes discover among Shabbir's belongings if for some reason the chiropractor can't personally direct the heroes to the mound.)

If Shabbir personally directs the heroes to the mound, the chiropractor indicates that it is impossible to gain entry during the day, due to potential discovery by nearby rangers, kids, and residual industrial traffic. Night is the only time that presents a reasonable chance at gaining entry unseen. If the heroes are on their own, even a simple reconnoitering of the area suggests the same thing. Heroes who refuse to see reason may still attempt to enter the mound, but an encounter with the security guard becomes unavoidable by day. While the first three encounters noted in the table below probably prove innocuous, the security guard, an employee of the West Virginia Ordnance Works, chases out trespassers, day or night, resorting to his .357 if attacked by unwise heroes. Use the Marginal-level Law Enforcer template in the *Gamemaster Guide* if necessary.

*d12	Encounter
1	d4 kids on a lark (excitable)
2	two lovers seeking solitude (curious)
3	one sandhill crane (hungry)
4	one Level 1 Combat Spec (security guard)
5–12	no encounter

* Roll d12 once per half-hour heroes spend in and near the TNT area—even if they are inside the burial mound, because there is no way to close it until they leave.

By night, an encounter can be startling, and open to false interpretation by paranoid heroes. Because of poor light, the heroes have incomplete information to work with during the first round of an encounter; whether it looks like a person or a animal, a dark shape suddenly flushed from behind a mound or seen approaching through the darkness may give heroes' hearts a lurch.

As noted on the TNT Area map, the burial mound, whose location is known only to Dr. Shabbir, is located past the edge of the TNT area, 100 meters into the forested McClintic Wildlife Preserve. To access the mound the heroes must pass through the TNT area, the road entry for which is chained off from the main road (Route 62) with a padlock. However, getting past the chain is as simple as walking over it (the area is a popular place for teens and young adults to party, park, and hang out), but driving a car in requires the PCs to pick the lock or cut it with a bolt cutter. Refer to the keyed entries below for additional descriptions, as the heroes move through the TNT area.

Bugged?

If the heroes are still unknowingly infested with electronic bugs (either from Scarborough's purse or the Sharp scientific calculator), their location in the TNT area is discovered by Balance soon after the heroes penetrate the mound. Because of AHD's past involvement with the area (described below), Balance is particularly interested in discovering why and how the heroes have come here.

With his matte black Bell Helicopter 206B JetRanger III in night/silent-running mode, Balance sets down near the burial mound after the heroes have entered. The heroes can make an Awareness–*perception* skill check. Those who succeed at the check see something dark and large dropping out of the sky (impossible to say what it is at a distance) and alighting upon one of the "igloo" mounds. The object darts straight up into the darkness an instant later, and is lost.

As soon as the helicopter touches down on one of the mounds closest to the burial mound, about 100 meters away, two junior AHD agents (called "handlers" in AHD lingo) emerge from the helicopter and set an ambush around the burial mound, ready to apprehend the heroes when they emerge. If heroes noticed the landing, they may meet the two handlers prior to the ambush. See "Ambush!" below for concluding this potential encounter, as well as the statistics for the junior agents, Agent Balance, and the helicopter.

TNT Area & Mound, Keyed Entries

Refer to the TNT Area map and the Burial Mound map for the following keyed entries. The buildings and other structures are all obviously long abandoned.

By day, the area is partially hidden from Route 62 by overgrown trees. However, several cars are usually pulled up along the side of the highway, near the chained entry road to the TNT area, and d4+4 curious visitors can be seen walking through the abandoned buildings.

By night, the buildings are hidden in darkness. Unless an encounter indicates otherwise, no cars are pulled up along the road. This is the best time for the heroes to attempt their raid on Cornstalk's lost grave.

North Power Plant. Only a cement and brick shell marks the location of what was once a power plant, according to the iron plaque still affixed to the structure.

South Power Plant. Another empty shell, this one without even a roof to screen out the elements. The original flooring is covered in a layer of hardened mud.

Fence. A rusted and half-fallen iron link fence surrounds the old "acid area." The broken, buckled roadway intersects the fence, and the gate that once blocked off the area lies in the weeds to the left of the road.

Ammonia Oxidation Plants. Both these buildings were once filled with terrifically dangerous chemicals and lethal fumes. Thankfully, only a few empty tanks, dozens of empty metallic drums, and the wind can be found in either of these buildings now.

Sulfuric Acid Concentration Buildings. Low cement buildings huddle in parallel rows, each accessible only through a single metal door. Though many of the doors remain locked and bolted, a few have been forced open during years of vandalism. The rotoevaporators and other equipment used to concentrate sulfuric acid, not to mention the end product itself, have been long evacuated.

Bunkers. These empty cement buildings stand open to the elements, devoid of content and contemporary purpose.

Igloos. During World War II, the intruding edge of the McClintic preserve was ripped up in order to construct one hundred "igloos." These large mounds of earth were shaped to be unnoticed from the air. Deep inside each mound, cement and steel protected the contents: wartime explosives. Tunnels once provided access between the igloos, but now the tunnels are collapsed, and the explosives are long gone.

McClintic Wildlife Preserve. These forested acres extend in all directions from the edge of the already reovergrown TNT area. Refer to the Lexicon for more information.

Burial Mound. Unless pointed out by someone already aware of the anomaly, the gradual swell of this mound is difficult to discern as anything other than a natural hillock on the edge of a forest. Even if noticed among the surrounding tree growth, the mound is easily taken for another earth-covered igloo of the nearby TNT area. In fact, it is something altogether different.

The mound is the secret grave of Chief Cornstalk. Though the errant pen of history indicates a burial elsewhere, in fact, tribesmen loyal to Cornstalk's memory interred him in this very mound and sealed it with Shawnee shamanistic magic. Only Shabbir's dedicated research into ancient Shawnee legends has retrieved the lost location from oblivion.

An entryway is not evident, even in the face of a vigorous search. Gaining entry requires the performance of the prescribed ritual, as described below.

B1. Mound & Entranceway

The lone hillock is thick with blue-bells and thorny scrub.

Short of access to a bulldozer and similar earth-moving equipment, penetrating the mound and accessing the burial chambers below is impossible via conventional methods. Vitalized by the surging Dark Tide, the method of gaining access is within the heroes' hands, if they can figure out a dream-culled clue.

Based on spiritual visitations, Shabbir has a sheet of paper on which is drawn a shaded circle, surrounded by seven additional concentric circles. Above the circles, a few stars are scattered. Shabbir knows only that the symbol somehow allows entry into Chief Cornstalk's mound. It is up to the heroes to discover the symbol's meaning, with some experimentation at the mound.

The shaded circle symbolizes the mound itself, while the seven surrounding concentric circles indicate that a visitor must completely circle the mound seven times (the direction is not important, as long as the direction is not reversed). The stars indicate that the mound can only be entered at night. If any being intent on entering the mound circles it seven times at any time past sunset, an opening appears in the mound's side as the last circle is completed.

The opening exudes the strong odor of new-turned earth. The orifice is only about 1 meter wide and 1.5 meters tall. Loose earth makes up the floor, walls, and even ceiling, through countless tiny rootlets are visible in the dirt.

The orifice appears even to those who haven't circled the mound. Should any hero happen to be looking at exactly the right spot as a companion finishes circling, the opening morphs into view in a manner not unlike a CGI effect in a modern movie. If any being conscious of the mound's significance circles the mound in the opposite direction of that used to open it, the orifice disappears. Otherwise, the entrance to the mound automatically disappears at the first flush of dawn. Anyone still within the mound is entombed alive. Kind GMs can allow trapped heroes to dig their way out over the course of a few desperate hours while the air grows stale, with a complex Strength feat check (5 successes, check once per hour).

Refer to the Burial Mound map cross-section on the interior front cover; the tunnel in the earth descends at a noticeable angle. The low ceiling and narrow tunnel make single file the only option for visitors. Heroes require artificial light (flashlights, Coleman lamps, and the like) while inside the mound.

B2. Entry Chamber

The tunnel opens up to either side and rises above, creating a rough earthen chamber some 4.5 meters on a side and 2 meters high at the center. A large granite boulder squats near the south wall. Faint flecks of paint on the stone recall an ambiguous design from ages past.

The warriors who buried their revered chief placed Cornstalk's prized possessions in this chamber, beneath the large stone. With a successful Social Science–*anthropology* check (at a +2 step penalty) or a successful Social Science–*history* check (at a +3 step penalty), the heroes note that the random designs painted on the stone are similar to ancient rock paintings discovered elsewhere, supposedly to convey the visionary experiences that shamans have while in a trance. A successful Investigate–*search* skill check calls out one ominous humanoid figure with wings and no obvious head, but with two glaring red eyes. Even heroes who find the gist of the painting meaningless can't help but note the painted arrow down the side of the rock, possibly pointing beneath it.

A successful Strength feat check at a +3 step penalty (other heroes can assist) is enough to budge the rock, should the heroes desire to do so. Unfortunately, a guardian spirit defends the rock. If the rock is rolled away, the invisible guardian spirit takes the physical form of a venomous snake, which darts out from "beneath" the stone. The cobralike snake bears a pattern on the back of its hood similar to random designs on the stone. If the snake is killed, the spirit vanishes and the snake reverts to the totem used to originally summon it: a length of knotted cords and beads.

If the PCs overcome the snake and search the hollow beneath the stone, they find the following items: three loose eagle feathers, a small bag with crystals and other stones, a small rattle carved with a human face, and a small tube of hollow bone. A successful Social Science–*anthropology* skill check indicates the possibility that these items once belonged in the repertoire of an ancient Indian shaman.

B3. Mid Chamber

The tunnel opens into another subterranean chamber. Four 2-meter-tall, 1-meter-wide concavities are visible in the walls, two on either side. Though shrouded in darkness, the concavities appear to contain skeletal humanoid forms.

At the very point where the contents of the depressions become partially visible, a field-effect from B4 (see below for details) temporarily scrambles any electronic equipment possessed by the heroes. Flashlights and battery-operated lanterns go out, cell phones go dead, and laptops crash (as do any electronic bugs), showing only a strange herringbone pattern. When plunged into darkness only a heartbeat after noticing the skeletal forms, even normally calm characters may panic. The GM is encouraged to play up this encounter, requiring bogus Awareness–*perception* checks and the like to simulate paranoid heroes blundering in the dark.

If calmer heads prevail, an alternative light source (such as a match or a lighter) provides sufficient light to see that nothing immediately menaces the heroes (although calling for another *per-*

Venomous Snake (guardian spirit)

STR	8	INT	2 (Animal 5)
DEX	10	WIL	10
CON	8	PER	1 (Animal 4)

Durability: 8/8/4/4   Action Check: 13+/12/6/3
Move: slither 24, creep 10   #Actions: 2
Reaction Score: Ordinary/2   Last Resorts: 0

Attacks
Bite (poisonous*) 12/6/3   1s/1w/d4w
   * The poison is a neurotoxin (see "Poison" in Chapter 3 of the *Gamemaster Guide*), insinuative, and modifies the victim's Constitution feat check to resist the poison with a +3 step penalty. The onset time is 1 minute.

Defenses
+1 resistance modifier vs. melee attacks
+1 resistance modifier vs. ranged attacks
Armor: d4–1 (LI), none (HI), d4–2 (En)

Skills
Stealth [10]–*hide [16]*; Stamina [8]–*endurance [12]*; Awareness [10]; Resolve [10]–*physical [12]*.

Kwakiutl Mask

Native North American cultures often carved and painted objects with patterns and symbols representing supernatural spirits. The objects were for giving thanks to spirits, to provide protection in warfare, and for more specialized purposes. The Kwakiutl Mask is very specialized—it allows its bearer to speak with mothmen, and the wearer commands their respect.

The wooden mask is very old. A stylized human face is carved and painted on the mask, however; a vertical seam bifurcates the face. Subtle hinges on the mask's side allow the outer face to open like a double door, revealing the inner, true mask. The inner mask is utterly black, except for two vividly painted red eyes. With the outer mask completely opened, each half resembles small stylized spread wings on either side of the dark face.

When wearing the mask (either by holding it in place, or affixing a strap), the wearer can see through tiny eye slits. If the outer face-halves are pulled open, the wearer is able to communicate in brief sentences with any mothmen who might be present. The power of mothman communication is a constant power.

For their part, mothmen recognize the mask as a sacred item important to their shamanistic tradition. They are favorably inclined to speak with the wearer, and to be friendly and accommodating (within reason). The wearer receives a –4 step bonus to all encounter skill checks when dealing with mothmen.

ception check to note "discrepancies" sustains tension). The field-effect from the innermost chamber is centered upon the entity located there (the mothman), and thus remains only so long as that entity remains (see B4). While the effect persists, heroes may attempt Technical Science–*juryrig* or *repair* checks to restore limited operation to electronic equipment. Even if repair is successful, restored operation is limited and liable to blink out again if conditions change (flashlights are only at one-quarter normal power, cell phones are anything but clear, and laptops are unreliable).

Four bodies reside in the wall, one to a concavity. These are the four former soldiers immediately responsible for slaying Chief Cornstalk over 200 years ago. Shawnee warriors avenged their chief's death by killing and interring the murderers here with the chief they slew. The bodies are strangely preserved, though their uniforms are nothing more than rotting remnants. Two of the bodies are wearing pistols. The antique flintlocks require significant cleaning and restoration, not to mention new ammo, should any hero desire to use them. Rough treatment causes the bodies to break and powder.

A flat stone in the floor contains the remnants of a crude scene depicted with stick figures. Four figures (the soldiers with their guns) stand over the fallen form of chief in full regalia, and the figure of a smaller individual. This painted stone is the record of the crime committed by the soldiers.

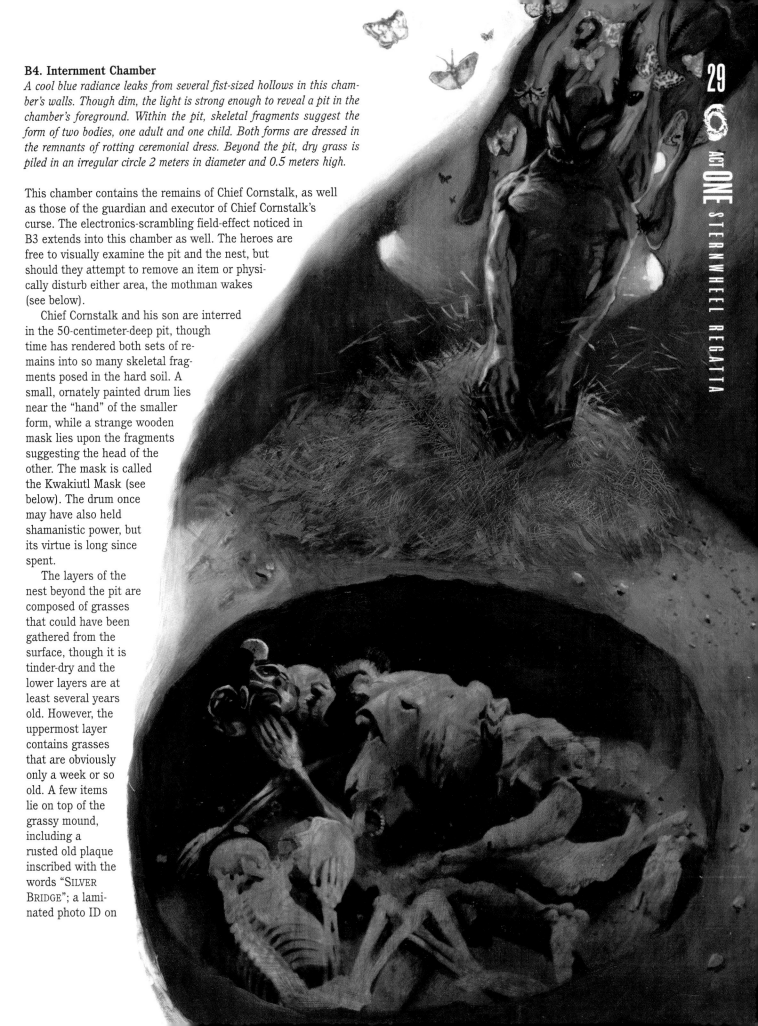

B4. Internment Chamber

A cool blue radiance leaks from several fist-sized hollows in this chamber's walls. Though dim, the light is strong enough to reveal a pit in the chamber's foreground. Within the pit, skeletal fragments suggest the form of two bodies, one adult and one child. Both forms are dressed in the remnants of rotting ceremonial dress. Beyond the pit, dry grass is piled in an irregular circle 2 meters in diameter and 0.5 meters high.

This chamber contains the remains of Chief Cornstalk, as well as those of the guardian and executor of Chief Cornstalk's curse. The electronics-scrambling field-effect noticed in B3 extends into this chamber as well. The heroes are free to visually examine the pit and the nest, but should they attempt to remove an item or physically disturb either area, the mothman wakes (see below).

Chief Cornstalk and his son are interred in the 50-centimeter-deep pit, though time has rendered both sets of remains into so many skeletal fragments posed in the hard soil. A small, ornately painted drum lies near the "hand" of the smaller form, while a strange wooden mask lies upon the fragments suggesting the head of the other. The mask is called the Kwakiutl Mask (see below). The drum once may have also held shamanistic power, but its virtue is long since spent.

The layers of the nest beyond the pit are composed of grasses that could have been gathered from the surface, though it is tinder-dry and the lower layers are at least several years old. However, the uppermost layer contains grasses that are obviously only a week or so old. A few items lie on top of the grassy mound, including a rusted old plaque inscribed with the words "SILVER BRIDGE"; a laminated photo ID on

Mothman (curse-addled)

STR	11	[+1]	INT	7	[0]
DEX	11	[+1]	WIL	13	[+2]
CON	11		PER	7	

Durability: 11/11/6/6   Action check: 13+/12/6/3

Move: sprint 22, run 14, walk 4, fly 44   #Actions: 3

Reaction Score: Ordinary/2   Last Resorts: 0

Attacks

Wing strike	5/2/1	d4s/d4+1s/d4+2s	LI/O
Talons	14/7/3	d4s/d6w/d6+1w	LI/O

Defenses

+1 resistance modifier vs. melee attacks

+1 resistance modifier vs. ranged attacks

+2 WIL resistance modifier vs. encounter skills

Immune to infection by *C. cnidarae*

Light Sensitivity: +1/+2/+3 step penalty in Ordinary/Good/Amazing light, respectively

Mutations

Field-effect (WIL) 13/6/3   special *(see text)*

Skills

Athletics [11]–*climb [12], throw [12]*; Unarmed [11]–*brawl [14]*; Acrobatics [11]–*fall [12], flight [14]*; Stealth [11]; Stamina [11]; Knowledge [7]; Awareness [13]–*intuition [14]*; Interaction [7].

This mothman hunter was summoned to the area over two hundred years ago at the behest of Cornstalk's dying curse, empowered by the magic of the Kwakiutl Mask. When Cornstalk's followers buried their chief, they buried the Kwakiutl Mask with him, ensuring that the mothman would remain in the area to guard the grave of the chief. The curse also imposed a kind of hibernation trance on the mothman, enabling it to sleep without need of food or water and without aging, until the mound is disturbed.

When wakened by external stimulus, the mothman ventures forth and engages in mischief. It was on one such excursion around fifty years ago that the creature came to the attention of

American Home Devices, Inc. (a company with an interest in the nearby ordnance works). Winged by a wild .22 bullet, the mothman fled southwest. Though the chase was nearly lost more than once, AHD agents only lost the trail for good after the mothman instinctively ducked into its old home territory: the deep spaces below Mammoth Cave. In time, the conditions of the curse reasserted themselves, and the mothman was forced to return to the burial mound. Later on, AHD agents discovered the secrets deep inside Mammoth Cave (described in Act Two, Scene Three). Forgotten, the original mothman continued its guardianship of the mound as it had for the previous century and a half.

Most recently, the mothman emerged to scare away a terminally ill and mentally delicate Jane Scarborough. After she fled, the mothman collected a few items she had dropped, adding to its collection of trophies. Constrained by the curse and the mask for two centuries and separated from its kind for the same time, the mothman has become little more than a vicious killing machine, and it gives the PCs no quarter.

Mutation: Field-Effect (WIL)

Several mothmen of the Mammoth Cave tribe carry this mutation, which explains the accounts of electrical equipment malfunctioning during mothman sightings in the area.

This mutation allows the mothman to create a 4.5-meter-radius field of influence that negatively affects most types of electronic equipment. Electronic lights simply fail, radios and cell phones only give static, and computer screens and other display devices show only a strange herringbone pattern. While the effect persists, a Technical Science–*juryrig* or *repair* skill check restores limited operation to affected electronic equipment. Even if successful, restored operation is limited (flashlights are only at one-quarter normal power, cell phones are anything but clear, and laptops become unreliable) and liable to blink out again if conditions change (subject to DM discretion). Equipment no longer subject to the field-effect operates normally.

A Will feat check is necessary to activate this mutation, which can be used three times per day. The degree of success determines how long the field-effect lasts: Ordinary: 1 minute; Good, 5 minutes; Amazing, 10 minutes. Note that certain precautions, including Faraday cages, can protect electronic equipment from this effect.

a chain with the company logo "AHD" above the picture of a young woman with the name Jane Scarborough; and a few pieces of notebook composition paper crumpled into a ball. Further bits of random debris lie in the nest, including a few rings, a rusted hubcap (at least thirty years old), and other oddments. All the items are caked with dried mud, as if they were somehow drawn through the earth. Hidden beneath the grass is a somnolent mothman—the famed "Mothman of Point Pleasant."

Any disturbance of the pit or nest, or an attempt to retrieve an object in either area, awakens the mothman beneath the grass. The creature rises from the dusty straw, its wings spread wide and its eyes glowing deep red. A resurgence of the field-effect at this point

shorts out any still-functioning electronics. If the heroes flee, the mothman follows. Unfortunately, PCs emerging from the mound may run right into a problem, as described in "Ambush!" below. A free-for-all ensues in this case.

Should the heroes secure and don the Kwakiutl Mask, the mothman flees and does not return until the PCs have gone. Also, heroes with FX abilities of their own may attempt to free the mothman from the binding curse. (Diabolism–*rend the weave* and Enochian–*unravel enchantment* would be useful in this regard, though both suffer a +3 step penalty due to the strength of the original casting.)

The mothman targets its attacks on heroes who are infected with *C. cnidarae*, if any. In the unlikely event that the mothman is presented with a living cnidocyte, it attacks that creature first.

Custom Bell Helicopter 206B JetRanger III

Using covert technology, AHD has refitted a few commercially available helicopters, converting them into instruments useful for industrial espionage and wetwork. In fact, these helicopters resemble to some extent those used by shadow organizations unsuspected even by AHD senior management, though those aircraft have even more advanced technologies.

The custom Bell Helicopter requisitioned by Andrew Balance has a silent-running mode. When activated, perfectly controlled audio interference waves cancel out the vestiges of rotor noise caused by air displacement. Painted matte black, the helicopter is outfitted for night running. The adaptive crystal optics incorporated into the cockpit windshield allow occupants reasonably clear night vision.

The helicopter is powered by an advanced prototype hydrogen fuel-cell engine that produces 420 shaft horsepower (when liquid hydrogen is burned to power the craft, only water vapor is the resultant exhaust). The standard Bell is a five-place aircraft, but with all the extra computer and audio generation gear necessary to compute and generate audio interference patterns, the custom Bell has seating limited to four people.

Because AHD doesn't want these custom helicopters to be associated with the company, no identifying marks can be found. Moreover, a switch on the dash activates a self-destruct mechanism that causes the helicopter to blow up in 30 seconds, just in case control of the helicopter becomes compromised. Questionable technologies are consumed in any such explosive inferno.

Specs: Acceleration 40; Cruise 110; Max 400; Durability 10/10/5; Armament .50 caliber mg (range 100/400/1000); Damage d6+1w/2d4w/d8m; Clip –/50.

Once the excitement subsides, the heroes have the opportunity to examine the mask, drum, ID, and ball of crumpled paper.

The photo ID is a vital clue for the heroes. It shows that Jane Scarborough was affiliated with a company called AHD prior to her theft of the heroes' car. Refer to Act Two, Scene One when the heroes have the opportunity to begin serious research concerning AHD.

If the heroes have the composition book, it's easy to see that these pages are those torn from the beginning of the book. The handwriting from the book is a perfect match with that in the loose sheets. Jane had been holding the pages in her hand, as a talisman against her fading memory, when the mothman emerged from the mound and she dropped them as she ran. A perusal of the handwritten text of the loose sheets provides the heroes with a glimpse into Jane Scarborough's life, plus a few interesting links.

Jane's "texts" and the sources of her research are not described, but nonetheless she was essentially correct. Sadly, she succumbed to the mental deterioration caused by *C. cnidarae* infection before she could execute her plan. Of course, even with the "talisman," (the Kwakiutl Mask), the particular mothman who had so long suffered the effects of Cornstalk's compulsion would have been unable

to help her. She would have had to journey to "the caves" after all. ("The caves" refers to the Mammoth Cave complex in Kentucky, but the heroes have no way of determining this except through investigation in Act Two.)

Note that Jane's mention of selling *C. cnidarae* technology to FEMA is only speculation on her part, though she was right to suspect a connection between AHD and the government, at some level.

Ambush!

As presented in "Bugged?" above, Agent Balance and two handlers set an ambush for the heroes, if the heroes are still electronically bugged. If the conditions are right, Balance silently sets his matte-black Bell Helicopter 206B JetRanger III down on a mound "igloo" closest to the burial mound, about 100 meters away. Balance remains in the helicopter while the two junior AHD agents attempt to set an ambush around the burial mound, ready to apprehend the heroes if and when they emerge. Unless

Barbara Davidson and Daryl Joslyn

AHD Security Specialists (handlers)
Level 6 Combat Specs

STR	10	[0]	INT	10	[0]
DEX	11	[+1]	WIL	10	[0]
CON	10		PER	9	

Durability: 10/10/5/5 — Action Check: 14+/13/6/3
Move: sprint 20, run 12, walk 4 — #Actions: 2
Reaction Score: Ordinary/2 — Last Resorts: 1

Attacks

9mm pistol	13/6/3	d4+1w/d4+2w/d4m
Unarmed	11/5/2	d6s/d6+2s/d4w

Defenses
+1 resistance modifier vs. ranged attacks
Battle vest: d6–3 (LI)/d6–2 (HI)/ d4–2 (En)

Skills
Athletics [10]; Unarmed [10]–*power [11]*; Modern [11]–*pistol [13]*; Stealth [11]–*shadow [12], sneak [12]*; Vehicle Operation [11]; Stamina [10]–*endurance [11]*; Knowledge [10]–*computer [11], deduce [11], language: English [13]*; Law [10]; Security [10]–*protocols [11], devices [12]*; System Operation [10]; Awareness [10]–*intuition [11], perception [12]*; Investigate [10]–*interrogate [11]*; Resolve [10]–*mental [11]*; Interaction [9]–*intimidate [11]*.

Gear
Bulletproof vest, 9mm pistol and ammo, shoulder holster, miniature radio with earpiece (1.5 kilometer range), sunglasses (tint varies with light conditions), stimulants, expensive Timex watch (electronically bugged)

They got me. Or, should I say, "I got it?" Doesn't matter, they gave it to me on purpose, and now I'm dying. Already, I'm thinking less clearly. Has to do with the infection. Bastards.

They think they'll find a cure, use the infection as a weapon, a threat. Sow terror, sell it to FEMA, who knows? Too late for me—I've burned those bridges, they'll never give me the cure now, even if they figure out how synthesize one. The captives aren't too cooperative. Don't blame them, I'd as soon gut as look at the bastards, myself. Too bad for the red-eyed buggers we captured, they're immune to the infection. Makes them ideal specimens from which to develop the cure, at least to the company's way of thinking.

I know something they've forgotten. They should look to their own history—I did. Yeah, the caves are the source of the infection. Home of the mothmen, too. But, 50 years back, the company would never have found the caves if they hadn't first run into "the mothman" in Point Pleasant. I did the research. I know.

I know . . . I can't think straight anymore, but it has to do with Cornstalk, and his curse. I know he had a talisman, the texts are clear. The talisman gave him power of the spirits—over mothmen! I know there is still a mothman out there in the TNT area, still bound by Cornstalk's last command. I can't get to the caves, that's the first place they'd expect me to run. But I can get to Point Pleasant. I can find the secret burial mound of Chief Cornstalk. When I get the talisman, when I can communicate with the mothmen, can a cure be far behind?

Please, God, I don't want to die.

the heroes are on their guard or are somehow aware of the ambushers ahead of time, the ambushers have one free phase of action.

The handlers aren't really interested in taking prisoners. They intend to quickly slay the investigators and bury them in the woods. If things go poorly for the ambushers, they attempt to break off the attack and retreat to the helicopter. Balance monitors the fight from the helicopter, and takes 1 round to fire his pistol at heroes who approach the helicopter (possibly in pursuit of a handler). He makes absolutely certain to take off before any hero can reach the helicopter, even if that means leaving both handlers behind. Balance is alone in the helicopter and can't both shoot and fly simultaneously. Perceptive heroes see Balance's sunglassed silhouette in the cockpit as the helicopter rises silently up and away (but might forget seeing this except under regression therapy, if Balance uses his telepathic talent to *obscure* his presence).

Wrap-up: Act One, Scene Three

As this scene draws to a close, the heroes have likely run into the mothman and either defeated it or chased it away. Hopefully, the heroes have learned that a company called AHD exists, that it is probably responsible for the *C. cnidarae* infection for which it is trying to find a cure, and that mothmen are also somehow involved. Heroes who take the Kwakiutl Mask from the burial mound will find it much easier to deal with a future encounter with mothmen (as is likely to happen in Act Two, Scenes Two and Three). Heroes who have been infected with *C. cnidarae* prior to this scene may be heartened by the knowledge about AHD's search for a cure and the mothman's immunity to this infection. Such heroes will continue to drive the plot forward for their own sake, apart from any possible assignment from the heroes' patron group. Information regarding AHD—possible research uncovered by the heroes, and the facility the PCs need to find—is presented in Act Two. Additionally, the appearance of mothmen should intrigue paranormal hunters, and Hoffmann Institute operatives are always interested in new information about other species.

If the heroes manage to subdue the mothman in the burial mound, their victory is short-lived. In fact, prior to leaving the mound, the mothman wakes and flees. If the creature is killed, the heroes now have a xenoform corpse on their hands! The manner in which the PCs deal with the body may have lasting repercussions on the campaign, but the GM has a number of ways to deal with the consequences. First, Hoffmann Institute agents should know better than to take the body anywhere but immediately to a Hoffmann safe house. Investigators who work for other agencies likely have their own protocols in place for such occurrences, as well. In the event that the PCs decide to "go public" with the body, however, the GM must take a more active role. Any number of circumstances can prevent the public at large from hearing about the body, including the following: a rival agency or government steals the corpse; anonymous figures offer the PCs obscenely huge bribes to forget the whole thing; a disinformation campaign by an agency of the GM's choice convinces the public that the body is a hoax; the PCs are attacked constantly until they change their minds about telling all; or any other limiting factor the GM devises.

Captured AHD black ops agents are well trained to reveal nothing to interrogators, regardless of the method of interrogation. The handlers demand to speak to their lawyer. If they are told they aren't under arrest but are still prevented from leaving, they loudly accuse the heroes of kidnapping. Should the heroes have paranormal means of gaining information from captured handlers, they discover the agents' real names (Barbara Davidson and Daryl Joslyn), and the fact that they are in the employ of AHD under the supervision of Lead Agent Balance, who also goes by the alias Jon Smithy. The receiver for tracking electronic bugs in the investigators' possession resides on the helicopter. Captured handlers are very dangerous to keep around, as they attempt to escape and carry out their original objective at the first possible opportunity.

Andrew Balance (Alias: Jon Smithy)

Lead Agent for AHD Security
Level 10 Free Agent

STR	10	[0]	INT	11	[+1]
DEX	12	[+1]	WIL	10	[0]
CON	12		PER	9	

Durability: 12/12/6/6
Move: 22/14/4
Reaction Score: Ordinary/2
Psionic Energy Points: 6

Action Check: 14+/13/6/3
#Actions: 2
Last Resorts: 2

Attacks

15mm sabot pistol*	14/7/3	2d4w/2d4+1w/d4+3m
Unarmed	11/5/2	d4s/d4+1s/d4+2s
Mounted in helicopter:		
.50 caliber mg	11/5/2	d6+1w/2d4w/d8m

* The sabot pistol is an item of superior technology, bearing no stamps or other identifying marks. Balance acquired it through a series of swaps with other shadow agency operatives. The weapon may be extraterrestrial in origin. It is a handheld electromagnetic accelerator that hurls a special rocket-slug at hypersonic velocities. Upon firing, a miniature scramjet ignites, accelerating the slug even faster. It carries five rounds in the magazine, plus one in the chamber. See Chapter 11 in the *Player's Handbook* for more information.

Defenses

Covert Armor* d6–1 (LI)/d6 (HI)/d6–1 (En)
* Covert armor looks and feels, to casual contact, like a black suit.

Skills

Athletics [10]; Heavy [10]–*direct fire [11];* Unarmed [10]–*power [11];* Modern [12]–*pistol [14];* Manipulation [12]–*lockpick [14];* Vehicle [12]–*land [13], air [13];* Stamina [12]–*endurance [13];* Computer [11]–*hacking [13];* Knowledge [11]–*deduce [12], first aid [12], language: English [14];* Law [11]; Security [11]–*protocols [12], devices [12];* Awareness [10]–*perception [11];* Investigate [10]–*interrogate [12], search [12], track [11];* Street–*net savvy [12];* Interaction [9]; Leadership [9]–*command [10];* Telepathy [10]–*obscure* [16].*

* Balance makes good use of his secret *obscure* ability to move into and out of places unseen or unremembered. Balance can sometimes selectively target memories of his victims, eradicating them if recent enough. See *obscure* in *Chapter 4: Arcana* of the DARK•MATTER campaign book for more details.

Gear

15mm sabot pistol, twenty-three scramjet slugs, covert armor, night-adaptive sunglasses (actually allows sight in full darkness to distance of 18 meters), a *Palm Pilot VI* (containing miscellaneous material, but including most of the heroes' real names, names of family members, employers, and other frighteningly private information about the investigators), a small leather case filled with lock-picking tools, a few dozen <devermis@yahoo.com> business cards, a magnetic card (allows access to every door in AHD Pharmaceuticals), *C. cnidarae* aerosol sprayer (see Act Two, Scene Three, room P28)

Act Two

640964565496 5240-500-0-2524524525
3252353265325235 5234562 545 255
35 5345235CNIDOCYTE4050853409585-43534543
345435346708983646643243-32592835682355
5328472184621498236598235325
53287653281563298534325-432524386732965321532532
598263587362598326593285623532454326
643
457457573657657
7567CNIDOCYTES98658
50101010101 10101010 100010 1
000111111

(The ancient folk with evil spells,

dashed to earth, plowed under!
--anonymous (north american indian))

In which the heroes' discovery of corporate misconduct leads to a secret lab where a terrible plague is being developed into a weapon of terror, and therefrom into the depths of the Earth.

Setting

Act Two of *The Killing Jar* is set in the state of Kentucky, called the Bluegrass State (capital: Frankfort). Like any large state of the union, Kentucky has many interesting cities and sights, including Fort Knox, the Daniel Boone National Forest, and Mammoth Cave National Park. Additional information about Kentucky can be gleaned from a common road atlas; however, unless the heroes become sidetracked, the details presented in this adventure suffice.

Although the heroes' research home base in Scene One isn't specified, at some point they will probably visit two important locations: Shelbyville, home of an AHD laboratory (Scene Two), and Mammoth Cave, the doorway to a larger subterranean world than most have ever imagined (Scene Three).

Scene One: Due Diligence

Before the investigators can move forward in their investigation, they must do some research. In Act One, the heroes learned that a company with the initials AHD is somehow involved with a horrible pathogen that killed Jane Scarborough. The same disease, *C. cnidarae*, may infect one or more of the heroes at this point.

Exactly where the heroes decide to find out more about AHD is unimportant. They may stay in Point Pleasant, or they may decide to head to a larger city for access to better resources. In any event, the heroes require the use of a library or the Internet to conduct their research, regardless of where they finally settle.

Researching AHD

A preliminary search for organizations or groups that use the term "AHD" either online, at a library, or through other methods available to the heroes produces a number of candidates for further investigation.

Present this listing to the players as a starting point for their heroes' investigations.

With the eight candidates in hand, the heroes face many phone calls, background checks, and other foot-to-the-pavement activities. Such research can be simulated through a complex skill check (7 successes, one check per hour) using the Investigate–*research* skill. If unsuccessful, additional research allows another complex skill check at one check per 2 hours, though more time gives Agent Balance additional opportunities to track the heroes down.

The more in-depth method of handling the necessary research calls for the players to play through the encounters, but the GM must also be up to the challenge. If the heroes hit on a particularly good, interesting, or even just fun strategy, the GM is encouraged to forgo game-mechanic simulation of pertinent re-

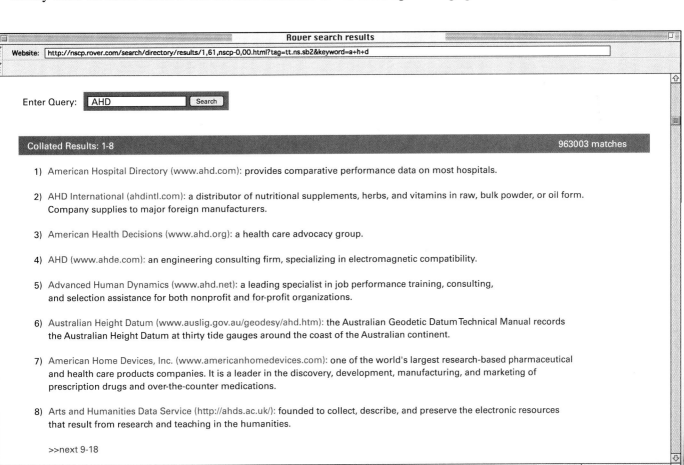

Rover search results

Website: `http://nscp.rover.com/search/directory/results/1,61,nscp-0,00.html?tag=tt.ns.sb2&keyword=a+h+d`

Enter Query: `AHD`   [Search]

Collated Results: 1-8   963003 matches

1) American Hospital Directory (www.ahd.com): provides comparative performance data on most hospitals.

2) AHD International (ahdintl.com): a distributor of nutritional supplements, herbs, and vitamins in raw, bulk powder, or oil form. Company supplies to major foreign manufacturers.

3) American Health Decisions (www.ahd.org): a health care advocacy group.

4) AHD (www.ahde.com): an engineering consulting firm, specializing in electromagnetic compatibility.

5) Advanced Human Dynamics (www.ahd.net): a leading specialist in job performance training, consulting, and selection assistance for both nonprofit and for-profit organizations.

6) Australian Height Datum (www.auslig.gov.au/geodesy/ahd.htm): the Australian Geodetic Datum Technical Manual records the Australian Height Datum at thirty tide gauges around the coast of the Australian continent.

7) American Home Devices, Inc. (www.americanhomedevices.com): one of the world's largest research-based pharmaceutical and health care products companies. It is a leader in the discovery, development, manufacturing, and marketing of prescription drugs and over-the-counter medications.

8) Arts and Humanities Data Service (http://ahds.ac.uk/): founded to collect, describe, and preserve the electronic resources that result from research and teaching in the humanities.

>>next 9-18

Website: http://www.americanhomedevices.com

This site contains information concerning AHD that may be useful to the company's customers, employees, and shareholders as well as the general public. In particular, AHD makes no representation or warranties as to the accuracy of any information contained herein and expressly disclaims any obligation to update said information. AHP further assumes no liability or responsibility for any errors or omissions in the content of this site.

CORPORATE OVERVIEW

NEWS

FAMILY OF COMPANIES

www.americanhomedevices.com
Questions? 1-800-123-2323

PRODUCTS

search in favor of roleplayed telephone conversations, face-to-face meetings, and other particulars. In every case but the seventh search element, this strategy requires the GM to invent the names of secretaries, company officers, and other personalities associated with the other completely innocent organizations, as necessary. For example, should the heroes decide to cold-call the American Hospital Directory, the GM should invent an automated answer system or a real receptionist, then a public relations officer, and possibly a human resources officer or maybe even a VP or CEO, depending on the particular hero's luck and skill in directing a conversation. Of course, in all cases but American Home Devices, the organizations are innocent no matter how deeply investigated, and representatives answer all questions to the best of their ability. The GM is also encouraged to concoct red herrings in the course of the investigation to further stimulate the players' (and characters') interest.

Making the Connections

The investigators may be able to identify both AHD and the target subsidiary, AHD Pharmaceuticals, through a series of methods and deductions not covered here, and the GM should be willing to accommodate these methods. However, the series of clues and tracks available to the PCs provides a clear path for deduction.

A good strategy for the heroes to identify their culprit involves a simple cross-referencing exercise. One important fact in the heroes' possession is the first key: The culprit organization was involved

with the TNT area near Point Pleasant during and immediately following World War II (noted under the Corporate Overview link in AHD's web page). None of the other companies can claim involvement in the West Virginia Ordnance Works; however, American Home Devices correlates with this fact, as detailed in AHD's website (presented below in text).

Once the heroes have identified AHD as the potential company serving as Jane Scarborough's former employer, discovering which branch of the gargantuan company she worked with allows the heroes to distinguish the guilty subsidiary from the uncompromised sites. The majority of AHD's divisions and personnel are completely innocent of conspiracy; only a few secret divisions are actively involved.

Heroes who confirm that AHD is indeed the company they seek via the TNT connection can zero in on the specific facility where Jane Scarborough worked. A computer phone directory search of all people named Jane Scarborough notes their location (a successful Knowledge–*computer operation* or Street Smart–*net savvy* check). Exactly one "Jane Scarborough" match (out of ninety-one) lists the home address as Shelbyville, Ky. Interestingly enough, a division of the already suspect company, AHD Pharmaceuticals, is located in Shelbyville (noted under the "Family of Companies" link in the AHD web page)!

Zeroing in on AHD

Visiting AHD's home web page is a great way for the heroes to gain an overview of the company's public front. It's also useful in uncovering additional contact information. Note that heroes may choose to access the website from a secure server, with cookies disabled, and/or have other security plans in place. Have the heroes roll any appropriate checks along these lines, though at this stage of the game, accessing the AHD website does nothing more than place a cookie on the heroes' browser identifying them as a new visitor. Of course, paranoid heroes may suspect far more sinister repercussions.

Among the information presented on AHD's main page is the ever-helpful 800 number, though the heroes may follow the other provided links before or after trying out the 800 number. The website is presented textually below, though the players should be encouraged to check out the AHD website for themselves if possible!

Corporate Overview: This link describes AHD as one of the world's largest research-based pharmaceutical and health care products companies. It is a leader in the discovery, development, manufacturing, and marketing of prescription drugs and over-the-counter medications. It is also a global leader in vaccines, biotechnology, agricultural products, and animal health care. The link goes on to claim that research and development is a top priority for AHD. Such has always been the case, as evidenced by its patriotic work during World War II, when it helped to maintain the Ordnance Works near Point Pleasant, W. Va.

News: This link displays a new series of headers tied to press announcements made by AHD, including declarations such as "American Home Devices Annual Meeting of Stockholders and Declaration of Common Stock Dividend," "American Home Devices Reports Sales and Earnings for the First Quarter," and "American Home Devices Announces European Approval of Lundicyx©, First in a New Generation of Drugs to Treat Insomnia."

Family of Companies: This link identifies several subsidiaries of AHD including Burke-Stull, Inc. (develops and markets herbicides, insecticides, and fungicides, located in Waterloo, Iowa); Ashton Development, Inc. (develops and markets popular over-the-counter drugs, including Advix©, Centrix©, Lundicyx©, and Robitussix©, located in Detroit); and AHD Pharmaceuticals (the general research and development arm of the company, located in the low-tax enterprise zone just outside Shelbyville, Ky.).

Products: Advix (pain medication), Centrix (multivitamin supplement), Lundicyx (sleep aid), and Robitussix (cough medication), but also over one hundred products in the areas of pharmaceuticals, consumer health care, agricultural products, veterinary products, and biotechnology. Many of these products should be familiar to the heroes. In fact, all of the heroes have probably used one or more of these products sometime during their lives.

800 Number: The 800 number dials AHD's corporate office, which is an automated system. Using the automated menu, investigators can discover all of the information attributed to the web page, including the location of every division.

At any time during the call, heroes may choose to press *1 and speak with an operator. Heroes who wait d20 minutes on hold (with lovely country tunes and the occasional "Your call is important to us, please stay on the line") are finally rewarded with a human voice. "Hi, this is Nancy in customer service. How can I help you?"

Nancy with AHD customer service is particularly unhelpful if the heroes do not have questions about a specific drug or other product produced by AHD and its subsidiaries. Nancy can't help the heroes with questions about company employees or other queries unrelated to consumer product information. PCs who persist in asking such questions are politely asked to "Please hold while I transfer you to Special Claims."

If "Special Claims" sounds ominous, it should. Overly curious, aggressive, or otherwise suspicious calls are always transferred to Special Claims. During the transfer, when callers are put on hold for about two minutes, standard operating procedure calls for a high-level trace on the offending call. A caller on hold can make an Awareness–*intuition* or Security–*security devices* check to recognize the possibility that a trace is being conducted. Should the heroes call from a previously secured location, AHD's high-level trace still may be able to penetrate it. Have the hero responsible for the secured line make a Security–*protection protocols* or *security devices* check to see if the trace is defeated.

A hero may hang up prior to the trace's completion should he or she become aware of it. If the characters do not tumble to the trace or choose not to hang up, a male voice finally picks up and says, "This is Special Claims."

The Special Claims Operator, as he calls himself, is terse and interested only in determining if the heroes belong to that special breed of potential troublemakers that a company such as AHD needs to worry about (a company that secretly engages in morally questionable, socially dangerous, and weapons-applicable research). The Special Claims Operator is initially suspicious (especially if the trace failed). Should the heroes choose to reveal their information regarding Jane Scarborough, strange organisms, or the like, the Special Claims Operator activates a task force to track down and deal with troublemakers quietly, though he tells the heroes only that "Your claims will be looked into. Please provide a phone number and an address where we can reach you." In fact, d4 handlers are dispatched to the trace location (or address, if given) in the guise of electricians, landscapers, or other innocuous disguises to arrange for a catastrophe, such as a gas leak, a furnace explosion, or a car bomb. Use the handler statistics provided in "Wrap-up: Act One, Scene Three" if necessary.

Wrap-up: Act Two, Scene One

As this scene draws to a close, the heroes should have a good idea about where they need to go to find to the truth: Shelbyville, Ky., home of the AHD subsidiary AHD Pharmaceuticals.

Scene Two: Shelbyville, Ky.

Coordinates:
Lat: 38° 13' 3" N
Lon: 85° 13' 52" W
Nearest Airport: Louisville International Airport
Population: ~6,500
Suggested Lodging: Wallace House Bed & Breakfast, Washington Street, Shelbyville KY 40065.

RANDOM SHOOTING IN LOCAL GROCERY

By Cheryl Gillie

SHELBYVILLE HERALD

JD Wiker, a former AHD-Pharmaceuticals lab technician, is sought in connection with the shooting at the Winn Dixie Food Store on Midland Blvd.

No arrest has been made, but police have "a good enough eyewitness account" to identify Wiker as the suspect.

According to eyewitnesses, the suspect snapped, rampaging through the cookie isle with a 12-gauge shotgun and a weed-whacker, attempting to blow away the unrighteous and trim them neatly down to a uniform quarter-inch depth—all while singing the "Old Navy Performance Fleece" jingle.

Though there were several injuries, no fatalities have been reported at this time. The suspect fled the scene and is currently at large.

Police say it isn't clear what prompted the shooting. Wiker's fellow shoppers, some of whom knew him personally, claim the AHD lab technician was always a very friendly, bubbly fellow. Says James Schubert, the grocery clerk, "He said he felt nauseous. A few seconds later, out came the weed-whacker."

Shelby County is known as the "Saddlebred Horse Capital of the World." Acres and acres of rolling hills, black fences, and horses of many breeds dot the surrounding landscape. A small town, Shelbyville has many small shops and businesses; however, due to the enterprise zone outside town (where the county hopes to lure in big business with low taxes and big incentives), the development of large retail and grocery outlets is already in progress. Many of the people who live in Shelbyville work among the new corporations and factories located in the enterprise zone. AHD Pharmaceuticals numbers among these businesses.

A Tangent

Heroes who specifically look at local papers or who make an Awareness–*perception* check notice the following story in the local paper, *The Shelbyville Herald*, which mentions AHD Pharmaceuticals.

In fact, JD Wiker was infected with *C. cnidarae*, and as sometimes happens with victims in the last stages of the infection, his mind became damaged. Fixating on a particularly annoying jingle, JD erupted into violence at the Winn-Dixie, then fled in his pickup truck, heading west. Several days after the time of the shooting (possibly after this adventure is concluded), police in Colorado discover the empty vehicle parked on the dam above Loveland, a small mountain town. JD is never seen again.

See "Zeroing in on American Home Devices" above if the heroes wish to question the company about JD Wiker.

Heroes who visit JD's former apartment (the telephone book provides the address) find it locked and empty. Police tape sealing the door indicates the place is under investigation. However, should the heroes break in, a successful Investigate–*search* check (at a +2 step penalty) reveals a hidden cache of guns, including three additional shotguns, two .357 magnums, and one submachine gun plus over d4×100 rounds of ammo for each weapon.

Heroes who interview James Schubert, the Winn-Dixie grocer, discover that except for a few superficial cuts, he is okay. Unfortunately, Schubert can only elaborate a little on his story. He says that earlier in the week, JD had come in for a pack of cigarettes. Based on a few comments JD let slip, Schubert concluded that JD was having trouble at work. Schubert, like everyone else in town, has nothing but good things to say about AHD Pharmaceuticals and indeed the entire enterprise zone, which has brought much needed growth to the small community.

Jane Scarborough

Questioning around the community reveals that Jane Scarborough is well known and liked. Common sentiment has it that Jane left on a professional sabbatical and is probably somewhere in Africa, on a camera safari. Calls to AHD Pharmaceuticals go unanswered (see below). Should the heroes locate and visit Scarborough's home (finding the address is as easy as looking in a phone book), they discover a modest ranch-style home. It is locked up; should the heroes gain entry, a search of the premises reveals a standard domestic setting, with the addition of a small library filled with substantial tomes dedicated to biology, chemistry, and biopharmaceutical research. Additional sections include substantial historical and art books featuring African and Native American lore (including one by Vernon Shabbir). A successful Investigate–*search* check turns up a loose sheet of paper in a Native American history book. The sheet of paper marks a section detailing the Battle of Point Pleasant (see the Lexicon under Chief Cornstalk). Written on the piece of paper are the words "Cornstalk's tool failed him, except in death. But that talisman will prevent my death if only I can find it and use it at the burial mound."

Shelbyville Police

The heroes may be tempted to bring their problems to the local police. This is a dangerous decision. AHD Pharmaceuticals has lined the local sheriff's pocket with enough cash to assure carte blanche operations out at the lab. In fact, Sheriff Branson and a few of his cronies respond to any alarm sounded at AHD Pharmaceuticals in d8+10 minutes, as described under the keyed entries for that area.

Sheriff Branson

Police Officer
Level 6 Combat Spec

STR	11	[+1]	INT	9	[0]
DEX	11	[+1]	WIL	10	[0]
CON	12		PER	9	

Durability: 10/10/5/5 Action Check 14+/13/6/3
Move: sprint 20, run 12, walk 4 #Actions: 2
Reaction Score: Ordinary/2 Last Resorts: 1

Attacks

9mm pistol	12/6/3	d4+1w/d4+2w/d4m	HI/O
Nightstick	13/6/3	d4+2s/d4+1w/d4+2w	LI/O

Defenses

+1 resistance modifier vs. melee attacks
+1 resistance modifier vs. ranged attacks
Bulletproof vest d6–3 (LI)/d6–2 (HI)/d4–2 (En)

Skills

Athletics [11]; Melee [11]–*bludgeon [12]*; Modern [11]–*pistol [12]*; Vehicle [11]–*land [12]*; Stamina [12]–*endurance [13]*; Knowledge [9]–*deduce [10], language: English [12]*; Law [9]–*enforcement [10]*; Security [9]; Awareness–*intuition [10], perception [11]*; Investigate [10]–*interrogate [11]*; *search [11]*; Resolve [10]; Interaction [9]–*interview [10], intimidate [10]*.

Gear

Police nightstick (club), 9mm pistol, handcuffs, battle vest, magnetic card (allows access to every door in AHD Pharmaceuticals)

The Shelbyville Police Department is located in a small building off Main Street. The building consists of a reception area, a large common office with ten desks, and one private office for Sheriff Branson. Down the security corridor are six small cells and a pink-painted drunk tank. A side door off the common office leads to the garage, big enough for five squad cars but usually containing d4–2 vehicles.

Besides the nonprofessional clerk/dispatcher (Alice Tully), the office usually only contains d4 police officers and Sheriff Branson. Heroes who come to the station with questions relating to AHD Pharmaceuticals are granted an appointment with Branson within a few minutes, in his office.

A big, beefy man, Sheriff Branson is a cordial listener. The sheriff listens to anything the heroes have to say and even attempts to draw them out further, seemingly out of a real concern for learning the truth. In fact, Branson attempts to assess just how much the heroes know. Should he decide they know too much, either by the certainty with which the heroes proclaim their beliefs or by their actually presenting evidence that incriminates AHD Pharmaceuticals, Branson takes action.

Feigning complicity with the heroes, Sheriff Branson says, "From what you've told me, I've got someone back in lockup who I think you need to talk to." Refusing to answer any more questions, Branson rises and leads willing heroes back to the drunk tank.

Should the heroes refuse to head back to the drunk tank, Branson sighs and pulls his police revolver. At the same time, he summons the d4 officers in the common office with a mere brush of his belt pager.

If the heroes fight, a blood bath may ensue. If the PCs wound or slay just one or two officers but escape, the surviving officers do not put out an APB on the heroes—they do not want a big investigation, which could potentially reveal their complicity with AHD. Unfortunately for the heroes, slaying even corrupt officers in a land of law is still murder. Should the heroes kill every police officer in the building, the PCs, though initially unidentified, become the focus of an FBI manhunt over the next few weeks. Graphic footage of the aftermath of the police-station slaying on national TV networks haunts heroes in the following weeks, but unless the GM wishes to develop a new adventure based around this development, allow heroes to use their Hoffmann contacts or other specialized connections to throw off concentrated pursuit. For reasons of its own security, AHD itself could call off the investigation.

Shelbyville Police Officers, d4

Police Officers
Level 4 Combat Specs

STR	11	[+1]	INT	10	[0]
DEX	10	[0]	WIL	10	[0]
CON	10		PER	9	

Durability: 10/10/5/5 Action Check 14+/13/6/3
Move: sprint 20, run 12, walk 4 #Actions: 2
Reaction Score: Ordinary/2 Last Resorts: 0

Attacks

9mm pistol	10/5/2	d4+1w/d4+2w/d4m	HI/O
Nightstick	11/5/2	d64+1s/d4w/d4+1w	LI/O

Defenses

+1 resistance modifier vs. melee attacks
Bulletproof vest d6–3 (LI)/d6–2 (HI)/ d4–2 (En)

Skills

Athletics [11]; Melee [11]–*bludgeon [12]*; Modern [10]–*pistol [11]*; Vehicle [10]–*land [11]*; Stamina [10]–*endurance [11]*; Knowledge [10]–*computer [11], deduce [11], language: English [13]*; Law [10]–*enforcement [11]*; Awareness [10]; Investigate [10]–*interrogate [11], search [11]*; Resolve [10]; Interaction [9].

Gear

Police nightstick (club), 9mm pistol, handcuffs, battle vest

AHD Pharmaceuticals

One square = 1 meter

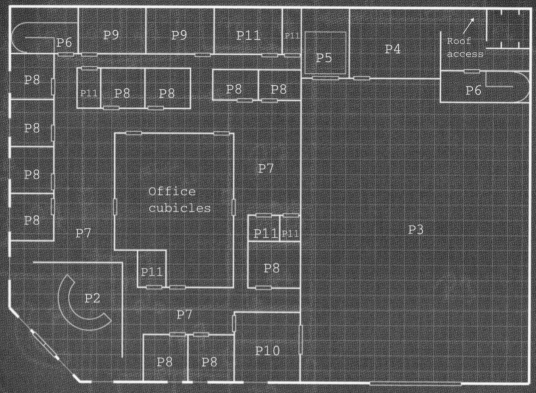

Main level

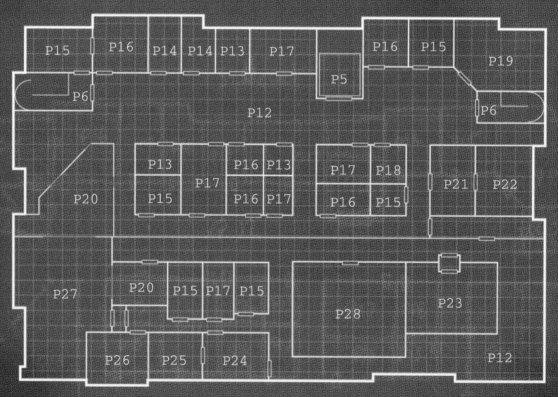

Sublevel

Currently, the drunk tank holds only Rusty, the town boozer, sleeping off a binge. Taking advantage of Rusty's chance presence, Branson points out the sleeping figure in the corner of the drunk tank as he unlocks the door, indicating the heroes should enter and speak with the figure, from which they'll learn the secret of what AHD Pharmaceuticals is really doing. Beneath its pink coating, the drunk tank is solid steel, and only a small view plate in the door allows sight (or bullets) each way.

If the heroes trustingly enter the drunk tank, it's locked tight behind them. Branson refuses to answer any questions and leaves. Poor Rusty knows nothing either way. Heroes may attempt to break out of the drunk tank, which requires a complex Manipulation–*lock-pick* check (4 successes at a +2 step penalty, one check per 20 minutes) to open the cell door. Unfortunately, 1 hour after the heroes are locked in, four white-clad AHD handlers arrive outside the door. Before the heroes are aware of the handlers' intentions, two knock-out grenades are tossed into the cell, spewing concussive waves (as soon as the grenades are thrown in, a steel panel over the view plate is closed from the outside, virtually assuring the heroes' loss of consciousness). Knockout grenades and handlers are listed below in "AHD Pharmaceuticals Keyed Entries," room P4, should their statistics become important.

Once the handlers are certain the heroes have been subdued, they enter the cell. Using gurneys, they transfer the unconscious heroes to the white van parked in the police garage, then to the AHD Pharmaceuticals facility and finally into one of the empty holding cells below the lab described under "AHD Pharmaceuticals Keyed Entries," room P22. If all goes smoothly, the heroes wake up in hospital gowns, devoid of their possessions and imprisoned.

AHD Pharmaceuticals

Located on a 5-acre plot backed up to a greenbelt, this single-story cement building appears drab and uninteresting. The facility exists on the edge of an industrial development consisting of several similar buildings; however, the other businesses are not involved with AHD, nor are they aware of any suspicious activity near or around the facility. Calls or a visit to the AHD Pharmaceuticals facility reveal the following message (on a prerecorded phone message and a small sign posted in front of AHD's driveway):

"Due to the recent tragedy, AHD Pharmaceuticals has temporarily closed its doors. The company is confident the investigation will clear AHD Pharmaceuticals from any connection with the actions of its former employee, JD Wiker. At that time, normal business hours will ensue."

The lab is temporarily closed, but the pending investigation is only a story to placate the local press and the many employees who innocently work at the site in administrative and support positions. Even though the business is ostensibly closed, the lower level remains partially online, where unprincipled researchers struggle with the puzzle of alien chemistries.

AHD Pharmaceuticals, Keyed Entries

When heroes decide that only a physical investigation of the facility will suffice, refer to the AHD Pharmaceuticals map, keyed to the entries below. If the heroes set off any alarms or come into view of a surveillance camera, refer to room P4, the Handlers' Depot.

Bugged?

Heroes who retain any form of electronic bug trigger sensors in the building, which in turn automatically transmits a message to Agent Balance. The black-ops specialist returns to the facility 2d4 hours after being notified of a possible security breach. Once back in the facility, he begins to track down any intruders, intent on ending their threat once and for all.

P0. The Grounds
A well-manicured lawn surrounds a low, gray building. A big parking lot stands empty in front of the facility. However, a door large enough to admit a semi suggests an interior garage, though the door is closed. The only other obvious entrance is set of large glass double doors accessing a lighted lobby.

AHD Pharmaceuticals Officials

The following information concerning AHD Pharmaceuticals is available to the heroes, should they spend some time looking through local newspapers and asking questions.

CEO: Larry Mahaffy
CFO: Patrick Gold
Spokesperson: Brad Demsy

Should the heroes attempt to confront the executives listed above, these company officials react with complete and convincing innocence. Accusations against AHD Pharmaceuticals trigger indignant denials of any wrongdoing. If the heroes make explicit claims but cannot offer proof, the executives dismiss the PCs outright and warn that any attempt to "leak" such allegations to the press will result in a slander or libel lawsuit. However, if the PCs can prove that they represent a powerful organization (any government agency or the Hoffmann Institute, for example) the administrators offer the PCs a tour of AHD Pharmaceuticals' interior labs to show that there is no basis for their claims. All protestations of innocence aside, these officers are fully aware of all AHD activities. If the heroes agree to a tour of the facility, they walk into a security ambush consisting of four handlers (or more, depending on the size of the PC group) waiting in the AHD Pharmaceuticals garage. The handlers' statistics are found in the garage entry, while the officials listed above can be considered nonprofessional administrators as described in the *Gamemaster Guide*.

Locked & Alarmed Doors

Two types of magnetic card readers secure the AHD Pharmaceuticals complex. The standard magnetic card readers respond to Jane Scarborough's key card. Without that card, the heroes face two checks: a complex Security–*security devices* check (3 successes, one check per minute) to bypass the alarm and card reader, and then a successful Manipulation–*lockpick* check with a +1 step penalty to open the door. If the alarm is not bypassed prior to opening the door, or should the heroes fail to disconnect the alarm, a low tone sounds that alerts the guards in the Handlers' Depot, room P4.

Advanced magnetic card readers protect certain areas in the building, as noted below. Without a special magnetic card available from the office of the CEO (P10), the heroes face a complex Security–*security* devices check (7 successes, one check per minute). As an added security feature, the card reader zaps would-be lock-pickers with d4+1s of electrical shock per failed check. As with the standard magnetic card reader, the heroes must also physically open the door with a successful Manipulation–*lockpick* check with a +1 step penalty.

Depending on secrecy as its best shield, AHD Pharmaceuticals doesn't maintain elaborately obvious guard systems. Still, a small video camera perched over the edge of the roof feeds a view of the parking lot to the Handlers' Depot, room P4, at all times (the PCs will automatically notice this if actively searching; otherwise, spotting the camera requires an Awareness–*perception* check). With a little care, heroes can evade the camera trained on the parking lot and slide up to the lobby doors or to the side or rear building walls.

Scaling the side or rear walls, which are just rough enough to enable such a feat without technical gear, requires an Athletics–*climb* check.

P1. The Roof

The tar roof is broken at regular intervals by vents, as well as by several antennas and a few miniature satellite dishes. Hidden from the ground below, the roof sports a 10-meter-diameter circular steel helipad painted with AHD's logo. A brick substructure provides an entry into the building, through a steel fire door.

Under normal circumstances, Agent Balance is on assignment and there is only a 10% chance that his matte-black Bell helicopter sits on the helipad. However, should the heroes attempt to penetrate the building, their proximity to special sensors alerts Balance and he returns to AHD Pharmaceuticals with all possible haste (see "Bugged?" above). Should the heroes trigger any sort of alarm while in the facility, Balance is also summoned and returns via his helicopter in 2d4 hours.

A standard magnetic card reader is mounted next to the fire door. If the heroes retain possession of the magnetic card originally found in Jane Scarborough's purse, they can gain access to the building's interior without setting off an alarm. Otherwise, refer to the "Locked & Alarmed Doors" sidebar. Once inside, stairs lead down to room P4.

P2. Lobby

Though lighted, the lobby is obviously deserted. Driving this point home is a "CLOSED" sign hanging in the glass of the lobby doors. Inside the lobby, a low counter backs up to an open wall prominently displaying AHD's logo.

A standard magnetic card reader is mounted next to the lobby doors, requiring either the use of Jane Scarborough's card or careful manipulation of the security system. The only item of potential use in the lobby is a list of interior extensions, showing approximately two hundred phone numbers. The various names listed include CEO Larry Mahaffy, CFO Patrick Gold, Spokesperson Brad Demsy, and Maintenance Supervisor Jon Smithy. Calls to the interior extensions of the first three names go unanswered, while a call to the fourth rings Agent Andrew Balance's cell phone. If he is not already alerted to the heroes' presence in the building, inexpert handling of the call could tip off Balance that something is not quite right back at the base.

Above the lobby counter is a smoked glass bubble, behind which lurks a security camera (Awareness–*perception* check to notice the camera). Each round the heroes linger in the lobby is a round longer that camera monitors in room P4 might notice the heroes and sound an alarm (see P4 for details).

The PA system is routed into the local radio station, WTHQ 101.7. Unfortunately, the PA system is a bit tinny and hollow, and the country music sounds a bit eerie as it plays in the darkened rooms and halls, especially since it can't be turned off here. (Heroes can use the all-page from any phone to temporarily supersede the music with announcements throughout the building, should they so choose.)

P3. Garage

A standard magnetic card reader is mounted next to the large garage door. Whether or not an alarm is sounded, the handlers described below take note anytime the garage door opens.

This dark, high space smells slightly of gasoline. Similar to any indoor parking structure, the garage floor maps out dozens of parking spaces in white paint. A half dozen spaces contain parked and empty cars of random make and model, all emblazoned with the AHD company logo. A loading dock against the far wall allows trucks or large vans to pull up directly to the back wall and unload or load cargo directly into a freight elevator. Currently, one white van, sans logo, is parked nearby. A door along the wall near the freight door stands open, and bright light streams from the opening.

The open door leads into the Handlers' Depot, P4. The sound of the garage door opening is enough to bring at least one handler still on duty to the door to see what's coming in.

As in most other chambers in the facility, country music softly plays over the PA, courtesy of WTHQ 101.7.

Customized AHD Van

The outward appearance of a generic, white-gloss van disguises the AHD all-purpose vehicle. With computer-assisted on-demand four-wheel drive and a customized suspension, the van can travel over most terrain, even mud, snow, or ice, and on grades too steep for other vehicles. The 6-liter, 300-horsepower V-10 provides wonderful acceleration (0–100 kph in 8 seconds).

The sidewalls of the van's tires are armored against weapon penetration, and the windows are bulletproof. A small antenna on the roof allows the van to track electronic bugs (such as those the heroes may have with them) on a state-of-the-art computer-GPS tracking system. Additionally, the passenger-side station of the front seat can toggle the release of a joystick triggering mechanism that raises a .50 caliber submachine gun from what normally appears to be a rooftop luggage box.

Besides the driver, up to four passengers can fit in the front two rows, which are separated by a retaining wall from the rear of the van. Each passenger station is equipped with a computer terminal (uplinked via satellite to the Internet), a bulletproof CF short coat (disguised as "painter's whites"), a bandolier of three knockout grenades, and one extra 9mm gun in the seat holster (see P4). Four radio headsets, a set of electronic picks, a set of regular picks, and other interesting tools can be found in a floor compartment.

Especially armored and electronically shielded, the rear of the van is ideal for transporting recalcitrant cargo. Besides fold-up gurneys and a plethora of leather tiedowns and bungees, the rear cargo space is empty. It locks from the outside, and all attempts to pick the lock suffer a +4 step penalty.

Specs: Acceleration 60; Cruise 100; Max 180; Durability 18/18/9; Armament .50 caliber SMG (range 100/400/1000); Damage d6+1w/2d4w/d8m; Clip –/50.

P4. Handlers' Depot

This small chamber seems to serve the triple function of locker room, duty station, and break room. Ten metal lockers, a shower, and related facilities are peripheral to the room, which also contains four bunkbeds, a large meeting table, and several computer stations.

A metal-rung ladder leads up to the roof, P1. The ten lockers are individually locked with combination locks that may be picked or forced. Inside, four of the lockers contain a black suit (reinforced polymer: d4–1 (LI)/d4–1 (HI)/ d6–3 (En)), a white "painter's" suit (with the same reinforced polymer), and an extra knockout grenade (see below)

Music does not play in this room. However, on almost an hourly basis the on-duty handlers make microwave popcorn, the buttery odor of which suffuses the area.

The computers are interesting from a security standpoint. They are not directly connected to the database containing the information the heroes need, though they do call out the existence of a "Secure Mainframe" and identify its location in the sublevel.

Strangely, the surveillance cameras for the sublevel are currently offline, though this doesn't bother the handlers—the cameras go offline every so often because of the strange field-effect surges that occur in relation to the research being conducted.

Four handlers are always on duty in this room, though more can be called in for special circumstances. One handler watches the computer screens, which are tied to the many interior surveillance cameras mounted throughout the building. The handlers question any PCs who make it into the garage without setting off an alarm, but heroes who have a good story ready and make a Deception–*bluff* check can get past the handlers without sounding an alarm. Of course, continued suspicious activity by the heroes (such as suspect behavior near a surveillance camera or having trouble operating a security card reader) once again draws the handlers' interest, and the second time probably results in the alarm being sounded.

For every round a hero appears within view of a surveillance camera in another part of the building, an on-duty handler has a

Handlers (AHD Security Specialists)

Kurt Fox, Beth Leach, Fred Zoeller, Arnie Hatter
Level 6 Combat Specs

STR	11	[+1]	INT	10	[0]
DEX	11	[+1]	WIL	9	[0]
CON	10		PER	9	

Durability: 10/10/5/5   Action Check: 14+/13/6/3
Move: sprint 20, run 12, walk 4   #Actions: 2
Reaction Score: Ordinary/2   Last Resorts: 1

Attacks

9mm pistol	13/6/3	d4+1w/d4+2w/d4m	HI/O
Unarmed	12/6/3	d6s/d6+2s/d4w	LI/O
Grenade	12/6/3	special (see below)	

Defenses

"Painter's" suit d4–1 (LI)/d4–1 (HI)/d6–3 (En)

Skills

Athletics [11]–*throw [12]*; Unarmed [11]–*power [12]*; Modern [11]–*pistol [13]*; Stealth [11]–*shadow [12], sneak [12]*; Vehicle Operation [11]; Stamina [10]–*endurance [11]*; Knowledge [10]–*computer [11], deduce [11], language: English [13]*; Law [10]; Security [10]–*protocols [11], devices [12]*; System Operation [10]; Awareness [9]–*intuition [10], perception [11]*; Investigate [9]–*interrogate [10]*; Resolve [9]; Interaction [9]–*intimidate [11]*.

Gear

"Painter's" suit, 9mm pistol and ammo, shoulder holster, miniature radio with earpiece (1.6 kilometer range), sunglasses (tint varies with light conditions), one knockout grenade

Knockout Grenade

Black box technology bundled into a small package, a knockout grenade produces concussive waves via an intense quantum oscillation. The wave inflicts d8+2s to targets within 1.5 meters of the impact detonation, d8s damage upon those within 3 meters, and d6s upon those within 9 meters. Intervening walls completely block the concussive wave.

chance to notice and sound the alarm. Roll an Awareness–*perception* check for a handler, modified by bonus or penalty steps, depending on the hero's specific actions while in view of the camera. Furtive or quick actions provide a +1 step penalty, while unconcerned strolls provide a −1 step bonus (as the handlers assume the character to be a researcher headed for the sublevel). The actual modifier is determined by the GM's assessment of the situation.

Should an alarm sound, either triggered directly by a handler or indirectly by heroes who smash a window or open a door without deactivating the security system, the handlers leap into action. From the moment the alarm sounds, three events occur, though their impact on the heroes occurs according to a staggered timeline.

First, Agent Balance is alerted to a problem at the facility. If not already en route, he flies to the facility in 2d4 hours to deal with the problem. Should Agent Balance find the heroes already gone, he makes tracking them to their current location his number-one priority (no more sending thugs, though he may enlist d4 more to help him). Balance's statistics can be found in "Wrap-up: Act One, Scene Three." If at all possible, the GM should see to it that any encounter with Balance ends with the black-ops agent getting away (possibly by using his *obscure* ability), making him available for a final encounter in Act Two, Scene Three.

Second, assuming nothing has happened to Sheriff Branson, he and two police cronies are alerted, and they drive over to the facility in d8+10 minutes. The sheriff has a master magnetic card, allowing him access to any chamber in the AHD Pharmaceuticals building. In this fashion, Branson serves as emergency backup for the handlers and Agent Balance.

Third, the four handlers mobilize, locating the heroes within the complex in d8 rounds. The handlers attack the heroes on sight. One throws a knockout grenade first, while the others open fire on intruders. Should the handlers capture some or all of the heroes, they are transferred to the sublevel, into a common holding cell (see P22), and their equipment is put into P21. Heroes who capture one or more handlers find them tight-lipped (see additional information regarding handlers' reaction to capture in "Wrap-up: Act One, Scene Three"). In any event, none of the handlers normally carries the specific magnetic cards used to access the lower level. They do know that such cards can be found in the office of the CEO (P10) should they personally need to head down into the sublevel in the event of an emergency.

P5. Cargo Elevator

The oversized elevator provides access between the main level and the sublevel. An advanced magnetic card reader is mounted next to the door, obviously of better design and security than those outside the building. Unfortunately, Jane Scarborough's card cannot bypass the lock, since her card's ability to access this level was terminated after her disappearance. (Bureaucratic oversight enabled her card to remain functional for the upper level.) Interrogation of captured or wounded handlers may reveal that a card capable of accessing the lower level can be found in the office of the CEO, P10. Sheriff Branson has such a card (as does the dangerous Agent Balance). Alternatively, heroes may forgo use of the card; see "Locked & Alarmed Doors" if they attempt to gain entry by force or stealth.

P6. Stairs

A heavy firedoor prevents unauthorized use of a flight of stairs with one landing that provides access between the main level and the sublevel. As in the cargo elevator (P5), an advanced magnetic card reader must be bypassed, either with the proper magnetic key or a direct attempt to thwart security and the lock.

P7. Office Environment

Black-trimmed office cubes fill open spaces, gray carpeting covers the floor, and white squares tile the ceiling. Currently, most of the lights are off, and only dim nightlights provide isolated puddles of light.

Little distinguishes the offices of the main level from offices the world over. Because of the building's temporary closure, the halls and cubes are empty, hollow. Faint strains of country music fill the halls, courtesy of WTHQ 101.7. The control for the PA is inexplicably tied into the mainframe of the sublevel.

P8. Offices

Several private offices are keyed to this entry, again entirely similar to offices found in other companies. They are devoted to human resources, personnel directors, requisition managers, and related occupations. Searches through these offices do not reveal anything suspicious or otherwise related to AHD Pharmaceuticals' real work. In fact, a study of all the available paperwork might lead one to believe that AHD Pharmaceuticals is involved in simple research aimed at finding new classes of antibiotics. The private offices are not immune from the music playing over the PA. Each private office has a 25% chance to contain a surveillance camera, keyed to P4.

P9. Restrooms

The restrooms are clean and smell strongly of rose-scented antiseptic.

P10. CEO's Office

A plaque on the locked door labels this the "Office of the CEO." Getting past the lock requires a Manipulation–*lockpick* check, although a surveillance camera linked to the monitors in P4 observes this office. Except for its size, little distinguishes this office from the other offices described in P8. However, a successful Investigate–*search* check reveals the CEO's spare magnetic key card, which hangs on a hidden hook beneath his desk. This key card allows access to the sublevels via the cargo elevator (P5) or the stairs (P6).

P11. Storage

Various-sized storerooms contain office supplies, lab coats, empty boxes and boxes full of old promotional flyers and other random junk, depending on the storeroom in question.

P12. Compromised Environment

Sparse night lights provide just enough light to see by, but little more—a few seem to be out, while others flicker intermittently. All the visible doors are wholly or slightly ajar. The wavering light reveals clean tile floors and antiseptically bare walls, although strange designs—hard to make out in the darkness—paint the floor and walls at random.

The worst has happened. With the near abandonment of the facility for appearances' sake, the carefully controlled experiments have escaped their "petri dishes." The strange patterns noted on the floor and walls are in fact spatters of blood, in some cases mixed with what appears at first glance to be drying mucus. The nearby doors that are ajar also bear traces of dried mucus at about knee height and on the handles. The few researchers and handlers who remained down here have been infected or killed. The heroes suddenly have more to worry about than the possible appearance of handlers, the sheriff, or even Agent Balance. Despite it all, WTHQ plays madly on.

While the heroes remain on the sublevel, roll d12 every 10 minutes to check for an encounter.

d12	Threat
1	Aibo XXIII Robotic Guard Dog (unique)
2	Tertiary cnidocyte (twenty-four total on level)
3	d4 tertiary cnidocytes
4	Secondary cnidocyte (six total on level)
5–12	no encounter

Aibo: The Mark XXIII Robotic Guard Dog, unlike the other threats loose in the sublevel, is one purposefully allowed to roam by the company. Developed under a side contract for military purposes from the commercially available Aibo (a robotic pet), the Mark XXIII is a robot designed for security. More to the point, it is vaguely dog-shaped, and its metal-toothed maw is for more than just show. Intruders are attacked on sight (regular employees are programmed into its database), but even strangers who brandish a high-level magnetic card can avoid attack. Aibo XXIII also has a smoked dome hiding a mobile surveillance camera in place of eyes, but because of the current blackout, the camera is not transmitting up to room P4 as it is supposed to. Similarly, the microphone and speakers relay and transmit only low-grade static. The mucus stains that cover Aibo's metallic muzzle look almost like the foam of a rabid dog, but actually are evidence of the robotic dog's encounters with cnidocytes.

Gamemasters concerned that the heroes are not experienced enough to deal with other threats on this level might consider allowing the heroes with a magnetic card to issue simple instructions to Aibo in order to augment their strength. In this fashion, Aibo makes a perfect ally, at least until the heroes' orders are trumped by Agent Balance.

Aibo XXIII Robotic Guard Dog

STR	14	[+2]	INT	9	[0]
DEX	7	[0]	WIL	7	[0]
CON	16		PER	4	

Durability: 16/16/8/8   Action Check: 10+/9/4/2
Move: sprint 18, run 12, walk 4   #Actions: 2
Reaction Score: Marginal/1   Last Resorts: 0

Attacks
Hydraulic Bite   d6+1s/d4+1w/d4+3w   LI/O

Defenses
+2 resistance modifier vs. melee attacks
Casing d4−1 (LI)/d4−1 (HI)/d4−2 (En)

Body Type
Processor: Good (5 active slots, PL 5); Actuators: Servo; Chassis: 2 m; Data Port: Telepresence link and uplink; Manipulators: None; Propulsion: Legs; Sensors: Rangefinder and video.

Skills
Stealth [7]–*shadow [9]*; Movement [16]; Stamina [16]–*endurance [17]*; Awareness [7]–*perception [9]*; Investigate [7]–*track [8]*; Resolve [7]–*physical [10]*, Security Devices [9].

Tertiary Cnidocyte

STR	4	(d4+2)	INT	2 (Animal 7 or d4+5)
DEX	10	(d8+6)	WIL	6 (d4+4)
CON	10	(d8+6)	PER	7 (Animal 7 or d4+5)

Durability: 10/10/5/5 — Action check: 9+/8/4/2
Move: undulate 6 — #Actions: 2
Reaction Score: Marginal/1 — Last Resorts: 0
Special: Only completely killed if burned. "Slain" cnidocytes otherwise recover full health in 10 days.

Attacks

Nematocyst sting* (×3) 10/5/2 1s/d4s/d4w LI/O
   * Sting: At the end of any conflict in which a hero has taken any direct damage from a cnidocyte, the victim must make a Constitution feat check at a +1 step penalty. Those who fail the check become infected with *C. cnidarae*; refer to the sidebar labeled "*C. cnidarae* Contamination" in Act One, Scene One for onset time and symptoms.

Defenses

–2 resistance modifier vs. melee attacks
Armor d6–3 (LI), d6–2 (HI), d4–2 (En)

Skills

Stealth [10]–*sneak [11]*; Stamina [10]–*endurance [11]*; Awareness [6]–*intuition [10]*.

Tertiary Cnidocyte: A number of tertiary cnidocytes have burst their containers, and roam singly and in small groups. See Act One, Scene One for the first appearance in the text, and the Lexicon for a more scientific treatise. Tertiary cnidocytes (fragments of secondary cnidocytes) often retain the shape of the form originally hijacked as follows (roll d4): 1) hand, 2) arm, 3) foot, 4) head.

Secondary Cnidocyte: Possessed of more intelligence than attributed to them by AHD, the secondary cnidocytes kept for research in the bowels of the lab burst their containers when the lab partially shut down. Timing their attack with an electromagnetic pulse instigated by a released mothman (P27), the cnidocytes have taken over the entire sublevel, with the few handlers in the main level none the wiser. Transparent ameboids like their smaller kin, secondary cnidocytes also retain vestigial forms of the large humanoid or animal that initially hosted the infection, but only as a source for the many tentacles now sprouting from the horror. The Lexicon contains some additional information (available to the heroes by way of the mainframe workstations in P25).

P13. Storage

Shelves on every wall hold boxes of lab supplies of every type, including latex gloves, water filters, petri plates, empty glass bottles, scalpel blades, wire, extra microscopes, and a hundred additional items. The chamber also contains an industrial-grade autoclave and glassware washer.

P14. Restrooms

The restroom is dark and apparently unoccupied.

Should any hero need to use or investigate the facilities, an Awareness–*perception* or *intuition* check prevents a nasty surprise. Tertiary cnidocytes lurk in the plumbing, one to each stall; see appropriate statistics above.

P15. Empty Lab

Ventilation hoods compete with lab benches for wall and floor space. Every flat surface is covered with bottles filled with myriad chemicals, petri plates, slides, notebooks, and equipment ranging from easy-to-recognize microscopes to rotoevaporators, gel electrophoresis plates, and chromatography columns.

   Simple observation reveals several tissue samples on petri plates and in cross-sections on slides. For heroes who take the time (10 minutes) to study any of the samples under a microscope or via the other more exacting methods available, a successful Life Science–*biology* check discovers that the tissue in the microscope, while organic, is not human. A Good or Amazing result on the check determines that there are two types of tissues, coming from two different but alien life forms (cnidocytes and mothmen, though the heroes won't know this).

   Heroes who take additional time (at least 30 minutes) to

Secondary Cnidocyte

STR	15	(d4+12)	INT	10 (d4+8)
DEX	15	(d4+12)	WIL	7 (d4+5)
CON	13	(d4+11)	PER	1 (Animal 1)

Durability: 13/13/6/6 — Action Check: 15+/14/7/3
Move: undulate 8 — #Actions: 3
Reaction Score: Ordinary/2 — Last Resorts: 0
Special: Only completely killed if burned. "Slain" cnidocytes otherwise recover full health in 10 days.

Attacks

Nematocyst sting* (×3) 15/7/3 d6s/d4+1w/d4m LI/O
   * Sting: At the end of any conflict in which a hero has taken any direct damage from a cnidocyte, the victim must make a Constitution feat check at a +1 step penalty. Those who fail the check become infected with *C. cnidarae*; refer to the sidebar "*C. cnidarae* Contamination" in Act One, Scene One for onset time and symptoms.

Defenses

+3 resistance modifier vs. melee attacks
–1 resistance modifier vs. ranged attacks
Armor: d6–1 (LI), d6–1 (HI), d6–1 (En)

Skills

Stealth [13]–*hide [18]*; Stamina [13]–*endurance [17]*; Awareness [11]–*intuition [14], perception [12]*; Resolve [11]–*physical [13]*.

peruse the many notebooks scattered around and who make a successful Investigate–*research* check learn much of the same information recorded for easy retrieval on the mainframe computer stations in P24.

A concerted search for Jane Scarborough's station and notebooks has a cumulative 20% chance to succeed in each of the five labs keyed to this entry. Jane's lab book is no different from the others at first glance; however, margin notes on several pages include short passages questioning the work, such as "I don't feel right about any of this," "I'm going to look into this, something isn't right," and "What does the company want with this research?"

P16. Inhabited Lab
Lab rooms keyed to this entry appear very similar to those described under P15, except for signs of vandalism. Glassware lies broken here and there, a ventilation hood is dented and sticky with some sort of slime, and some machines mysteriously continue to run, though no operator stands nearby. In fact, released cnidocytes prowl this chamber: Roll for an immediate wandering encounter (see P12). Aibo can be encountered here, assuming the heroes have not already met and neutralized him.

P17. Collections
These chambers are labs similar to P15, but even a quick look indicates these areas have considerably more damage than P16. An Awareness–*perception* check reveals two feet sticking out from beneath an upright freezer in one room, an arm protruding from a floor cabinet in another room, and other signs revealing the location of some of the research staff who didn't leave when the lab was shut down.

Investigation reveals researchers in lab coats, still living and breathing, unceremoniously stuffed in and beneath lab equipment. One researcher can be found in each of the rooms keyed to this entry (a total of five). Each is the victim of multiple cnidocyte stings, as is apparent by slimy residue, puffy skin, and red welts where stung. They all are suffering from accelerated cases of *C. cnidarae* (see P28). Each victim has a magnetic card allowing access to the elevator and stair doors.

If roused (requiring a successful Knowledge–*first aid* or Medical Science–*treatment* check), infected researchers moan and mumble, but are unable to form coherent sentences. They stumble along after heroes who lead the way, but at the first sign of a cnidocyte or a mothman, they scream bloody murder and run away in a random direction. All researchers suffering from *C. cnidarae* succumb and perish in d12 more hours, though the bodies continue their transformations. . . .

P18. Embattled Technician
The first thing a hero notices upon passing these doors is that they are closed and locked, unlike most others in the sublevel. In fact, a lucky technician named Duncan Hinkle managed to barricade himself in this lab (similar to P15) before being stung by escaped cnidocytes. Attempts to unlock the door (a successful Manipulation–*lockpick* check) bring a crash and hoarse screams to "Get away from the door, you damned monsters! GET OUT!"

Hinkle, a graduate from the local high school recently hired to work at the facility, is terrified beyond the capacity for rational thought. Heroes who open the door must make a successful Interaction–*charm, interview,* or *intimidate* check to dissuade Hinkle from braining the first hero through the door with a 2-liter glass solvent bottle. Should the heroes calm Hinkle down without too much fuss, the technician gratefully accompanies them, too afraid to leave their sides but constantly stressing the need to get out of the building. Because of Hinkle's inexperience, he can't really help the heroes, except to point them toward the solvents room (P19), where he does most of his work.

P19. Solvents
This well-ventilated chamber contains several dozen varieties of solvents, including methanol, ethanol, acetonitrile, and dichloromethane. Many large drums line the east wall, while the rest of the space is taken up by 2-liter bottles of various solvents on shelves.

The solvents are mostly organic-based chemicals used in a variety of laboratory procedures. Each drum stores approximately 100 liters of chemicals and is too heavy to move easily. This place is not amenable to sparks, matches, or any sort of open flame: Solvents are as flammable as gasoline, and are also poisonous if contacted or inhaled. Treat short-term inhalation or contact (up to 10 rounds) as an irritant poison with an immediate onset time and a duration equal to the length of contact (see

Duncan Hinkle
Nonprofessional

STR	8	[0]	INT	10	[0]
DEX	9	[0]	WIL	9	[0]
CON	9		PER	9	

Durability: 9/9/5/5   Action Check: 10+/9/4/2
Move: sprint 16, run 10, walk 4   #Actions: 2
Reaction: Marginal/1   Last Resorts: 1

Attacks

Unarmed*	8/4/2	d4s/d4+1s/d4+2s	LI/O
Solvent bottle**	9/4/2	d4+1s/d4w/d4+1w	LI/O

    *+d4 situation die
    **or whatever is handy

Defenses
None

Skills
Athletics [8]; Unarmed Attack [8]; Melee [8]–*bludgeon [9]*; Vehicle Operation [9]; Stamina [9]; Knowledge [10]–*computer [11], language: English [13]*; Physical [10]–*chemistry [11]*; Technical [10]–*juryrig [11], repair [11]*; Awareness [9]; Interaction [9]–*bargain [10]*.

Gear
Lab coat, lab goggles, gas mask

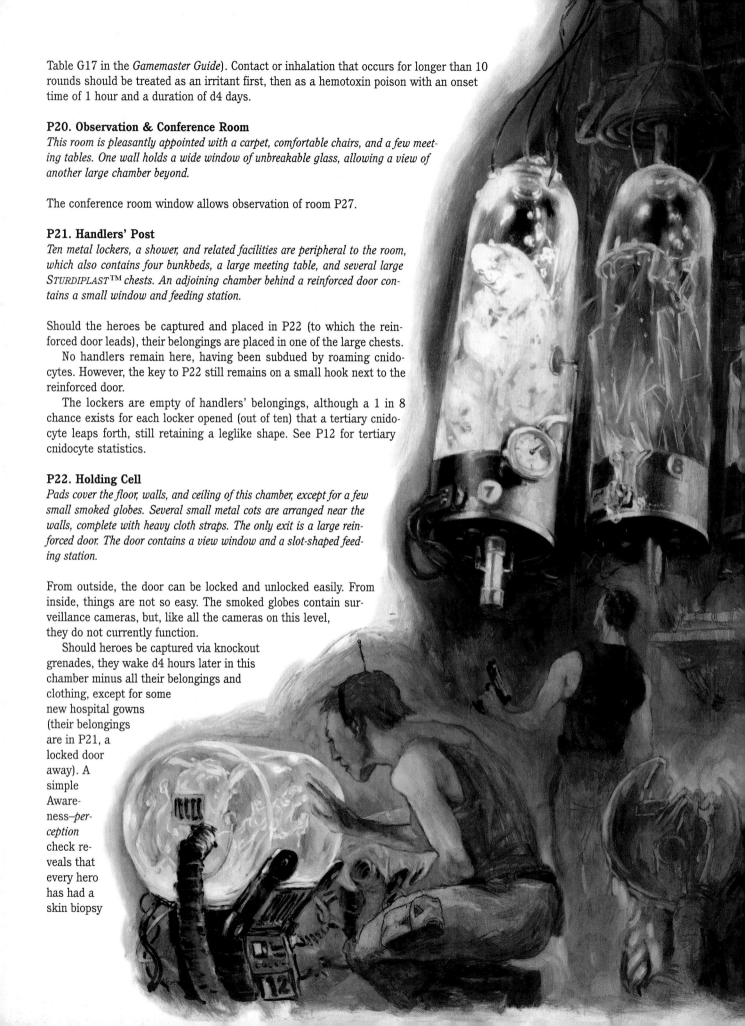

Table G17 in the *Gamemaster Guide*). Contact or inhalation that occurs for longer than 10 rounds should be treated as an irritant first, then as a hemotoxin poison with an onset time of 1 hour and a duration of d4 days.

P20. Observation & Conference Room
This room is pleasantly appointed with a carpet, comfortable chairs, and a few meeting tables. One wall holds a wide window of unbreakable glass, allowing a view of another large chamber beyond.

The conference room window allows observation of room P27.

P21. Handlers' Post
Ten metal lockers, a shower, and related facilities are peripheral to the room, which also contains four bunkbeds, a large meeting table, and several large STURDIPLAST™ chests. An adjoining chamber behind a reinforced door contains a small window and feeding station.

Should the heroes be captured and placed in P22 (to which the reinforced door leads), their belongings are placed in one of the large chests.

No handlers remain here, having been subdued by roaming cnidocytes. However, the key to P22 still remains on a small hook next to the reinforced door.

The lockers are empty of handlers' belongings, although a 1 in 8 chance exists for each locker opened (out of ten) that a tertiary cnidocyte leaps forth, still retaining a leglike shape. See P12 for tertiary cnidocyte statistics.

P22. Holding Cell
Pads cover the floor, walls, and ceiling of this chamber, except for a few small smoked globes. Several small metal cots are arranged near the walls, complete with heavy cloth straps. The only exit is a large reinforced door. The door contains a view window and a slot-shaped feeding station.

From outside, the door can be locked and unlocked easily. From inside, things are not so easy. The smoked globes contain surveillance cameras, but, like all the cameras on this level, they do not currently function.

Should heroes be captured via knockout grenades, they wake d4 hours later in this chamber minus all their belongings and clothing, except for some new hospital gowns (their belongings are in P21, a locked door away). A simple Awareness–*perception* check reveals that every hero has had a skin biopsy taken. Of far more concern, every hero not already suffering from *C. cnidarae* infection who fails a Constitution feat check is now infected. See P12 for tertiary cnidocyte statistics and information on the illness's progression.

Strangely, the heroes' captors are nowhere to be found. The heroes are alone, locked in a compromised sublevel, left to their own devices to escape.

The reinforced door is solidly locked; opening it requires a complex Manipulation–lockpick check (3 successes, 10 minutes per check) by a hero using some form of needle or pin. Of course, finding a needle or pin in the chamber is the hard part. If the heroes cannot think of a way to escape the trap in a way that meets with the GM's approval, things look grim. Thankfully, the terrified Duncan Hinkle—looking for aid from anyone still alive—can free the heroes (see P18).

The heroes' potential for interaction in this area requires the GM to keep careful track of time. If either the police or the AHD handlers capture the PCs, the cnidocytes do not escape their cages until the characters are safely contained in this chamber. If the heroes make their way directly to this sublevel without being apprehended, they run directly into the escaped cnidocytes.

P23. Cnidocyte Containment

Two steel doors guard entry to this chamber. The prominent magnetic card reader and the "airlock" between the exterior and interior chambers demonstrate the scientists' desire to secure the interior chamber. However, both doors now stand wide open.

Stainless steel plates this large room. Two-meter-tall metal and glass containment vessels line the walls, while at least twice as many half-meter-tall vessels march in long rows down the center. The vessels all resemble incubators for premature newborns, except for their varying size. Flashing lights line the bases of many of the vessels, apparently displaying interior temperature, humidity, and more obscure data. The glass fronts of many vessels are fogged by humidity, but despite the translucency, it seems that some of the largest containers may contain people.

About half of the vessels, both large and small, are smashed open, dark, and empty. The floor near these vessels is slick with clear, gelatin-like smears.

AHD Pharmaceuticals researchers kept their live cnidocyte samples in this "animal" facility. With the shutdown, six secondary cnidocytes and twenty-four tertiary cnidocytes burst from their containment vessels and now roam the entire sublevel. A count reveals six intact large vessels (which hold secondary cnidocytes) and thirty unbroken small vessels.

Smashed vessels of both types are empty except for a disgusting slimy residue. Once the moisture is wiped away, it's easy to see the large vessels contain humans infected with *C. cnidarae*, well on their way to complete transformation (most are already dead, and their flesh is beginning to slump and fade into transparency). These people were mostly collected from among the unmissed homeless of nearby large cities (Chicago, Philadelphia, Lexington, and St. Louis), and their names are not recorded by AHD (instead, lab notebooks merely assign them an Incubation Host Number). For each vessel investigated, the appropriate hero must make a Personality

feat check to simulate luck—a failed check indicates an awakened secondary cnidocyte, which bursts through the glass the next round.

The small incubation vessels contain human hands, heads, and feet, as well as whole rabbits, rats, cats, and other small animals, all of which are nearly or completely transformed into tertiary cnidocytes. A hero who investigates a small vessel and fails a Personality feat check will see and feel the sudden jerk and struggle of a tertiary cnidocyte trying to get out; however, none of these creatures can escape without the aid of the larger secondary specimens.

Besides the incubator vessels, a small countertop in the room's center holds several sealed liquid nitrogen vats. Each vat contains frozen samples of *C. cnidarae*, collected both from samples in the room and from something labeled "PRIMARY SOURCE."

P24. Computer Station

Comfortable chairs are gathered around a central island on which several personal computers are situated, quietly displaying innocuous screen savers.

These workstations are tied directly into the server-mainframe, and will allow the heroes access to several pieces of information important to their investigation and potential cure. Any successful computer related skill is sufficient to find a wealth of information regarding AHD Pharmaceuticals activities. Many directories contain completely harmless biological research into prosaic proteins; however, a directory on the desktop prominently labeled PROJECT MOTHMAN is a clear indicator of something special. Computer-savvy heroes note that the directory is actually pulled from another computer called Mainframe, which physically resides in the next room, P25. None of the information from this directory can be copied, duplicated, or printed.

The target "MOTHMAN" directory contains eight subdirectories:

Overview: This subdirectory contains a few documents. The subdirectory's analysis document sums it up succinctly: "AHD Pharmaceuticals, a subsidiary of American Home Devices, Inc., is under contract to produce a unique bioweapon. The contracted bioweapon will be suitable for wide dispersal for purposes of urban subdual. Said bioweapon will also be useful for specific application vs. individual dissidents, troublesome political icons, and journalists or investigators that cannot otherwise be dealt with. The threat of application of said bioweapon could also become a workable avenue for social and individual control."

The name of the institution or group that contracted AHD Pharmaceuticals does not appear here.

C. cnidarae: The following summary appears among several related documents (including documents that report findings similar to those noted by Dr. Kline in Act One, Scene Two). "The organism in question bears a resemblance to those of the phylum Cnidaria, yet contains structures unlike any thus far known to biologists. The organism has therefore been named *Clostridium cnidarae*, for obvious reasons. *C. cnidarae* are not microorganisms according to the generally accepted definition, because of their large size. If the infectious agent is allowed to infect natural fauna, the victim is slowly killed as it transforms into a lifeform not native to the earth's surface. The resulting organism resembles a gargantuan jellyfish and is often referred to as a secondary cnidocyte. If large sections of the secondary cnidocyte are removed, those sections sometimes maintain independent mobility and are called tertiary cnidocytes. The *C. cnidarae* infection itself was harvested from the Primary Source. The primary organism's phenotype remains a topic for speculation."

Cnidocyte, Secondary: Several documents of basic biological function research are summarized by an analysis: "Secondary specimens originate in earthborn fauna when the *C. cnidarae* infection is allowed to run its course. The resulting organism resembles nothing so much as a man-sized jellyfish or freshwater hydra. Note that the organism is extremely dangerous, but with proper precautions in place, it is a promising specimen for our ongoing bioweapon goals."

Cnidocyte, Tertiary: Several documents of basic biological function research are summarized by an analysis: "Tertiary cnidocytes originate when a secondary cnidocyte splits or is purposefully bisected. Though smaller than secondary cnidocytes, tertiary cnidocytes are dangerous infectious organisms and should be handled with extreme care."

Status: This subdirectory contains several hundred documents, representing the compilation of research from lab notebooks of the primary researchers. A document labeled "Analysis" contains pertinent summary information: "The sample obtained from the Primary Source has proved suitable for the bioweapon project's goals. However, the continued inability of the research team to synthesize an inoculation or cure specific to *C. cnidarae* is problematical. Thankfully, the team believes that time is the only barrier to the development of a vaccine, in light of the demonstrated immunity of the xenoforms found living in proximity to the Primary Source."

Xenoforms: This directory contains a variety of documents. Most are witnesses' accounts of mothman sightings of the past. The associated analysis document summarizes, "Though xenoform sightings are reported in several areas associated with North American native burial plots, AHD research has discovered a colony of the xenoforms colloquially known as 'mothmen' occupying an extensive but natural subterranean cavern system, codenamed PELLUCIDAR. At this time, the only defined access to Pellucidar is through a company-sponsored "test plot" leased from Mammoth Cave National Park, Ky. As was demonstrated in the lab and in the field, the xenoforms are immune to the effects of *C. cnidarae*. Due to an unfortunate incident at first contact, the xenoforms are ill-disposed to aid in our research. Despite this, several live specimens have been collected and are the focus of intensive immunological research. We strongly suspect the xenoforms are fully aware of a cure for the *C. cnidarae* infection, and if we could establish friendly relations, an immunological option might be immediately forthcoming. But what is not given freely can be taken."

An accompanying .GIF file provides a clear map of the AHD's private entrance into Mammoth Cave (see the Mammoth Cave National Park map in Act Two, Scene Three).

Primary Source: This directory contains only a single document, titled "Speculation." Excerpts from the document include the following: "Severe upheaval accompanied the powerful New Madrid earthquakes that struck during the winter of 1811–1812. By winter's end, few houses within 420 kilometers of the Mississippi River town of New Madrid (Missouri) remained undamaged. Survivors reported that the earthquakes caused cracks to open in the earth's surface, the ground to roll in visible waves, and large areas of land to sink or rise. Damage was reported as far away as Charleston, W. Va., and Washington, D.C. Frontiersmen near what is now called Mammoth Cave National Park reported plumes of dust geysering from known cave entrances. Based on our physical survey, as well as our research based on files acquired from the Vatican Z-database, we believe that the New Madrid earthquake was the side effect of a DOORWAY opening and closing below the ground. Something came through, but for unknown reasons it apparently returned whence it came. We refer to this visitor as the Primary Cnidocyte. Residue left by the visitor in the form of *C. cnidarae* remains viable even after 200 years, and this forms the basis of our bioweapon research. The xenoform 'mothmen' found near where we retrieved the biological residue reacted poorly to our sample collection, and they remain a dangerous deterrent to deeper probes that might determine if a Doorway truly exists in the vast subterranean spaces riddling the North American continent."

Developments: Several documents are contained in this subdirectory, mostly research notes into possible avenues of biological research for *C. cnidarae*. The "Analysis" document reads: "Despite the failure to date in finding a viable cure, several possibilities for dispersal (via drinking water, air dispersal, or specific injection) and acceleration of desired effect have been demonstrated. With the addition of an engineered enzyme, victims of the accelerated *C. cnidarae* strain succumb to death in a matter of hours, not days, as is true for exposure to the native organism. The fabrication lab has developed prototype aerosol dispensers with the accelerated strain. This is an exciting breakthrough, for several reasons. Affected organisms undergo rapid necrotization and liquefaction, without ever developing mobile secondary or tertiary characteristics associated with the unmodified *C. cnidarae*. In this, we've developed the ability to eradicate a population without repercussions and while leaving the underlying infrastructure intact. If left undisturbed, target organisms are reduced to so much anonymous organic powder, which conventional forensics is unprepared to handle. The disconnection of secondary and tertiary ambulatory development is an obvious improvement. Finally, victims of the aerosol-delivered strain show marked suggestibility prior to final necrotization (2 to 8 hours). This unlooked-for side effect could provide us with additional revenue, as methods for mind control seem to be perennially popular."

P25. Mainframe

A large mainframe is the obvious focus of this computer lab, although spare chips, wires, modems, and other components are stored here as well.

On the mainframe resides the delicate information presented in the previous entry. A hard-wired terminal provides direct access to the mainframe. From this terminal, operators can directly access much of the machinery in the building. Strangely enough, it is only from here that WTHQ can be switched off, dousing the building in heavenly silence. The "blackout" responsible for the surveillance camera and radio disconnection can also be reset here with a Computer Science–*programming* success. A similar check allows the operator to manually control distant surveillance cameras and the surveillance camera attached to Aibo XXIII.

Any attempt to copy, print, or port the sensitive information regarding Project Mothman requires the proper password (which is Alhazred, but there is probably no way for the heroes to know this). Only a successful complex Computer Science–*hacking* check at a +4 step penalty (6 successes, one check per minute), allows the data to be duplicated or transferred. Even then, another complex Computer Science–*hacking* success with the same penalty is required to deactivate a Trojan virus, which erases all the data and crashes all connected hardware within 24 hours of duplication.

On a failure to copy or print the data, security protocols initiated long ago kick in. In order to protect sensitive data and AHD's reputation, a self-destruct countdown quietly begins, visible only as a small digital readout in the lower left part of the screen, beginning at 15 minutes and working its way down. See the next entry for additional details in this event.

P26. Power Plant

The iron doors, stenciled with the words "Power Plant," are securely locked with a cutting-edge padlock (a successful Manipulation–*lockpick* check at a +3 step penalty is needed to open it).

An ominous cylindrical metal device is mounted on iron clamps in the center of the chamber. The vaguely bullet-shaped apparatus sprouts a jumble of wires that snake into a hole in the floor.

AHD Pharmaceuticals draws all the power it needs from the local utility company, so what's the deal with this room? It's not a power plant, it's insurance. In case AHD Pharmaceuticals is compromised, a well-designed firebomb provides proof against later incrimination. This room holds only the main portion of the device; charges are also set throughout other sensitive areas of the building. The firebomb can be initiated via a remote signal from the CEO, Agent Balance, or unnamed officials of the parent company, AHD, should the need arise. The firebomb is also set to go off if security measures described under P25 are activated. Once the countdown starts, it can only be delayed (with a successful Security–*security devices* check) by an additional 5 minutes. When detonation finally comes, the resulting fireball erases all evidence of AHD Pharmaceuticals' moral transgressions.

Heroes could trigger the countdown themselves directly at the source, if it is not already initiated, with a successful Demolitions–*set explosives* check at a +2 step penalty.

P27. Xenoform Lab

A series of two steel doors allow entry to this chamber, over which is stenciled the words "XENOFORM LAB." Judging by the prominent magnetic card reader and the "airlock" between the exterior and interior, it seems security was considered important for this chamber. A rack inside the "airlock" contains two cattle prods, utilized by AHD researchers to keep the mothmen at bay while they draw blood and skin samples. Currently, both doors stand wide open.

This large chamber is reminiscent of a large zoo exhibit. Poured rock textured to resemble natural stone creates a faux cavern, complete with a few stalactites, a waterfall, and a small central pool. The illusion is ruined by what appear to be thin metal strips that underlie the entire room like striations in the poured rock. Several dark figures lie strewn on the rocks, and one lies half submerged in the central pool.

The six figures look like robed men from a distance, but closer scrutiny reveals the robes as furled wings—the figures are dead mothmen! From the hundreds of stings that cover each body, it is possible to guess the truth: These mothmen, defenseless and trapped in the "exhibit," were killed by rampaging cnidocytes. Trails of slime confirm it, though no cnidocytes apparently remain anywhere within the chamber.

Cattle Prod
Melee–*powered*; En/O; d4+1s/d4+3s/d6+4s; Clip size: 20.

The thin metal strips are a sort of Faraday cage, which usually prevents the mothmen from using their field-effect powers to disrupt conditions in the lab. Even with the insulation, the mothmen still manage the feat on a fairly regular basis.

The Faraday Cage effect (named after its discoverer) means that the electric charge on a conductor sits on the outer surface of it. Therefore, no electrostatic field is present within the conductor. It is basically a metal screen-wire enclosure all wired together electrically and grounded, with continuous walls, floors, and ceilings and therefore no openings for EMF to get in or out. The door is solid metal and has fuzzy or solid copper seals all around it to maintain the continuity of the structure. A single cage can be as small as a basketball, or large enough to enclose a building.

The mothman lying facedown and half submerged in the central pool is not dead yet, as is noted by a simple Awareness–*perception* check: The mothman's chest continues to move as if the creature were still breathing. Unfortunately, the associated pool hides the transparent form of a secondary cnidocyte. When the mothman is pulled out or turned over, the cnidocyte simultaneously leaps out of the pool at the nearest hero, providing a perfect opportunity to scare the PCs. See P12 for secondary cnidocyte statistics.

When the heroes drive off or destroy the cnidocyte, the remaining mothman regains consciousness. Still, the heroes are hated beings, representatives of the race responsible for its current condition, and it shrinks from contact unless the PCs have the Kwakiutl Mask. If the heroes display the mask and initiate communication, the mothman relates the following in a dry, whispering voice:
- Selfish humans (AHD scientists) stole members of the Tribe (mothmen) from their caves (Mammoth Cave).
- The Formless (cnidocytes) are evil and are not of the Earth. The Tribe eradicates the Formless whenever encountered, so that the sanctity of the Earth is not compromised.

- The Formless came from deeper in the Earth, deeper even than the ways hunted by the Tribe.
- Those of the Tribe are not subject to the corruption of the Formless, and they know the secret to bestowing that immunity, even to those not of the Tribe.
- The Kwakiutl Mask is the physical evidence of the pact between ancient humans who lived with the Tribe below the earth long ago. If the heroes bring the mask into the earth, the Tribe will honor that pact and provide a cure for any heroes suffering from the taint of the Formless.

The mothman gasps out its answers with increasing distress. It is near death; unless a hero makes a successful Medical Science–*treatment* check at a +3 step penalty, the mothman perishes shortly after giving out its information. In the unlikely event that the heroes manage to save the mothman's life, it remains in a comalike stupor for the next two weeks. Heroes who wish to take the creature back into the world had best use the utmost discretion in order to avoid unwelcome attention. If necessary, refer to the mothman statistics in Act One, Scene Three.

If the heroes have no real impetus to visit Mammoth Cave on their own (for instance, if none are infected with *C. cnidarae*), they might still wish to return the ailing mothman to its home and thereby initiate contact with the "xenoforms." In this case, the mothman doesn't require such heroic efforts to keep it alive, but lingers in a coma until it can be tended to by its own kind.

See "Wrap-up: Act One, Scene Three," for the possible consequences of heroes acquiring a mothman corpse.

P28. Fabrication Lab

The clutter typical of a machine shop fills this chamber. Heavy tools of every type are racked on walls and mounted to heavy benches. Implements to cut, pound, flatten, stretch, and shape metal, wood, plastic, and glass are obvious. Also present are large bins of spare parts, including metal sheets, plastic and rubber tubes of every gauge, and a wall of electronic parts more complete than the inventory at Radio Shack.

AHD scientists assemble prototype implements here. Heroes with any facility in Technical Science can find a tool for most any job here, and possibly the parts to accomplish it. Heroes who desire to do so can take precious time to repair their own equipment or cobble something together—all Technical Science checks and other checks deemed appropriate by the GM proceed with a –3 step bonus.

The guts of several promising projects are strewn about here and there, but a glass case holds the fabrication lab's best prototypes. The case contains one Cnidarae aerosol sprayer, one environmental monitor, and one pulse baton. All the items are well constructed, but are obviously not "machine tooled" as a mass-produced item would be. Indeed, these items show weld seams, scratches, and other obvious signs of prototype construction.

Wrap-up: Act Two, Scene Two

The heroes are close to the cure they need, either for themselves or the Hoffmann Institute (or similar organization). With a map (the .GIF file) showing AHD's "test plot" and special entrances into the area below Mammoth Cave, and possibly with the assurance of their one mothman contact, the heroes are in for some spelunking.

If the heroes got into and out of the facility before Agent Balance arrived, or if the heroes encounter him without ending his threat, Agent Balance tracks the heroes to Mammoth Cave. Even if the heroes have discovered the electronic bugs, Andrew Balance can put the facts together to easily deduce the heroes' next stop, espe-

Environmental Monitor

Advanced sensors developed at other AHD labs are incorporated into this handheld PDA. With the incorporation of the new sensors, the monitor not only tracks contacts, email addresses, and appointments, it also monitors local atmospheric pressure, humidity, temperature, and electrostatic charges. This information allows the user to project a picture of current weather trends, allowing weather to be accurately predicted 12–48 hours in advance with a successful Knowledge skill check at a –2 step bonus.

Pulse Baton

This device looks like a modified cattle prod. Because of the increased charge it delivers, it comes complete with special insulated gloves that must be worn by the operator to avoid accidental charge leakage.
Melee–*powered*; En/O; d8s/d4+2w/d6+2w; Clip 20.

Cnidarae Aerosol Sprayer

This sprayer looks something like a fat-barreled pistol. Where the hammer would be on a conventional pistol, the sprayer sports a battery-cooled glass bulb, which is filled with distilled *C. cnidarae* in a solution of nitrogen and special enzyme accelerants. Only AHD Pharmaceuticals can produce this solution, and the only viable batches exist in this sprayer and Agent Balance's prototype, each holding enough solution for about five shots.

Any creature struck by a burst of aerosolized, enhanced Cnidarae solution (resolved as normal for a ranged weapon) must make a Constitution feat check. On a Failure, the victim internalizes the accelerated *C. cnidarae*. The modified infection goes to work immediately. Unless he or she has access to the cure known only to the mothmen of Mammoth Cave, the victim dies in 2d4 hours. In the time leading up to death, the victim becomes disoriented and unstable. If presented with a strong command or order, the victim must make a Will feat check or follow the order to the letter, to the best of his or her ability. When death comes, the victim's physical body liquefies and drains into so much anonymous slime in just d4 hours. Due to the modifications to the Cnidarae organism, the victim's body doesn't reanimate as a cnidocyte.
Modern Ranged Weapon–*pistol*; Range 5/10/20; no physical damage (but see above); Clip 6.

cially if he can view the computer security logs indicating which files the heroes accessed. Even without accessing such files, Balance knows they have an ancient Indian artifact relating to the mothmen, and he knows the mothmen may be hiding a cure. Balance is nothing if not an expert extrapolator.

Balance notes the disarray of the facility and realizes the heroes have likely escaped with damaging information that links AHD with unethical activities. Making a command decision, he triggers the firebomb in P26, setting it to detonate in 15 minutes. He uses this time to make a clean getaway. If the heroes are still somewhere inside the building, all the better. Should Balance be taken out of the picture by expert heroes, a late-arriving black-ops agent from another arm of AHD shows up to do the job. At the GM's option, this same agent takes up where Balance failed and tracks the heroes to Mammoth Cave.

If AHD Pharmaceuticals is cleared out and blown up and no hero is infected with *C. cnidarae*, a trip into the bowels of the world may not seem like such a great idea. Some heroes may very well balk. Of course, Gamemasters who railroad their players run the risk of alienating them; however, the use of lures is a great option. In this case, possible lures include dreams of foreboding experienced by psionic heroes; reports of unusual seismic activity noted in journals or online by Tech Op PCs; or an outbreak of *C. cnidarae* that threatens a group or an individual known to the heroes (making finding a cure even more important). The Hoffmann Institute (or other appropriate organization) is naturally very interested in learning more, and will offer generous bonuses to those willing to undertake a journey into the earth.

Scene Three: Mammoth Cave, Ky.

Coordinates:
    Lat: 37° 11' 55" N
    Lon: 86° 8' 50" W
Nearest Airport: Warren County Airport
Suggested Lodging: Diamond Caverns Resort & Go; Mammoth Cave Parkway Rd., Park City KY 42160.

Mammoth Cave National Park is Kentucky's number-one tourist attraction, with close to 2.5 million visitors per year. On the surface, Mammoth Cave encompasses acre after acre of forested ridges and valleys, filled with flowers, trees, birds, hiking trails, deer, and many other natural wonders. Of course, the big draw is the underground cavern network, which is mapped at over 283 kilometers, though experts agree that it is probably much larger. A few nuggets of additional information can be found in the Lexicon.

Heroes visiting Mammoth Cave can take advantage of lodging, sights, and tours offered by the National Park if they desire. Of course, none of the official entrances on park maps easily connect to the caverns below AHD's test plot.

The easiest way to the plot (refer to the Mammoth Cave National Park map) is via West Entrance Road (Highway 70). According to the map, AHD's test plot lies at the end of Joppa Ridge Road. A road atlas also provides additional cues to the park's geography, but those details are not important to the core adventure.

Heroes may speak with Mammoth Park rangers in order to obtain general park information or to query officials about AHD and its plot. Ranger Philippe Faribault, attached to the main Visitor Center, agrees to meet the heroes and answer any questions they may have. Ranger Faribault knows the following:

- AHD's test plot is primarily concerned with cultivating endangered species of foliage and wildflowers indigenous to lower Kentucky. AHD claims some of these plants may have pharmaceutical properties. The lease helps defray a portion of the park's annual expenses. Faribault is pretty sure there is not a cave entrance below the test plot (of course, he's wrong).
- The terms of AHD's lease are such that the park does not have authority over anything that might occur on the land leased by AHD for the term of the lease, which is in its fifth 10-year contract. However, AHD has never done anything to make the park officials suspicious or concerned.
- While Mammoth Cave has a more diverse and populous ecosystem than any other cave in the world, there is no evidence of creatures larger than bats, crickets, crayfish, springfish, salamanders, and spiders (wrong again).
- Stories are told of crackpots who tried to live down in the cave system. There was even a whole colony in the 1800s, but that failed. However, people native to the area over two thousand years ago explored the cave system, and even today, newly (re)discovered sections show evidence of occupation by these Archaic Americans (evidence includes arrowheads and simple cave drawings).
- Most experts think that the cave is only about twice as large as is currently mapped, but a few think that the cave system was once far, far larger until connections to the larger system were sealed off during the New Madrid earthquake (see Act Two, Scene Two, P24).
- Should the heroes convince Ranger Faribault that they believe something is not right at the AHD test plot, Faribault either issues a warning against trespassing, or, if the GM thinks the heroes could use a hand, agrees to accompany the heroes to the site. In this fashion, Faribault becomes a short-term ally. When the ranger realizes that AHD has discovered a new entrance to the caves and has kept that information to itself, he is incensed. Should Faribault personally encounter mothmen and other marvels of the new system, he counsels the heroes to keep their discoveries under wraps, to "preserve the wonder of this unsuspected natural ecosystem." Plus, he admits wryly, it is doubtful that anyone but "new age weirdoes" would believe stories of subterranean civilizations.

AHD Test Plot

The gravel Joppa Ridge Road winds through forested ridge tops and valleys, finally ending at the entrance of a plot of land surrounded by barbed wire. Inside the fence, a fairly level expanse of land is apparently planted with several varieties of flowering shrubs, bushes, and flowers. Through the gate, a driveway winds through the flowers, apparently heading toward a large greenhouse. Behind the greenhouse, a small building is also visible.

Ranger Philippe Faribault

Level 6 Tech Op

STR	8	[0]	INT	12	[+1]
DEX	11	[+1]	WIL	12	[+1]
CON	10		PER	7	

Durability: 10/10/5/5   Action Check: 13+/12/6/3
Move: sprint 18, run 12, walk 4   #Actions: 2
Reaction: Ordinary/2   Last Resorts: 0
Perks: Fortitude (–1 step bonus to *endurance* checks)
Flaws: Code of Honor (respect for natural world)

Attacks

7.62mm rifle	12/6/3	d6+1w/2d4+1w/d4+1m	HI/O
Unarmed*	4/2/1	d4s/d4+1s/d4+2s	LI/O

    * +d4 base situation die.

Defenses

+1 resistance modifier vs. ranged attacks
+1 INT modifier vs. encounter skills
+1 WIL modifier vs. encounter skills

Skills

Athletics [8]–*climb [12], jump [9]*; Modern [11]–*rifle [12]*; Vehicle [11]–*land [13]*; Movement [10]–*swim [11], trailblazing [11]*; Stamina [10]–*endurance [11]*; Survival [10]; Knowledge [12]–*first aid [13], language: English [15], language: French [15]*; Life [12]–*biology [13]*; Physical [12]–*geology [13]*; Animal Handling [12]; Awareness [12]–*intuition [13], perception [13]*; Investigate [13]–*track [14]*; Resolve [12]; Interaction [7].

Gear

7.62mm rifle & ammo, watch, backpack, personal radio, bedroll, flashlight, survival gear, first aid kit, binoculars, climbing and spelunking gear

---

In fact, AHD really is growing and tending a variety of threatened plants, because they believe that there might be pharmaceutical money in the development of particular unique proteins associated with some of the flowers. A Life Science–*botany* check reveals threatened and endangered plant species including Tall Hairy Agrimonia, Western Silvery Aster, Western False Foxglove, Yellow Lady's-Slipper, French's Shooting Star, Eggert's Sunflower, Wood Lily, Hairy Nutrush, and Wood's False Hellebore, among others.

Two (of the four) researchers assigned to the site, Christine (Chris) Hill and Nelson Kuniansky, are AHD botanists concerned with the noble sentiments publicly ascribed to the test plot. These researchers can be found out among the test plot fields or greenhouse by day and sleeping in the bunkhouse by night—the other two are not encountered until the heroes descend into the cave system. The two aboveground researchers are initially friendly to any visitors to the test plot. Under questioning, the botanists reveal the following:

- Two additional researchers are assigned to the site, Ken Allgier and Mike Wiles, but they are not usually around because of a special project.
- A successful Interaction–*charm* check by the heroes entices Chris and Nelson to reveal that AHD has hit on another entrance to Mammoth Cave, and that Ken and Mike spend most of their time exploring. The two botanists are not in on AHD's secret, and if the heroes express sufficient curiosity, they may be allowed to see the entrance (see the greenhouse below).
- If Ranger Faribault accompanies the heroes, or the heroes can come up with a reasonable story as to why they should be allowed to enter the "new" cave entrance, Chris and Nelson acquiesce.
- Heroes who act with criminal disregard or threaten the botanists come under suspicion; at the first possible opportunity, one of the botanists uses a cell phone to call the state police, who arrive on the scene 45 minutes later. If the police are summoned, they will not enter into the cave entrance, but wait outside for heroes and attempt to arrest them for criminal trespass.

Bugged?

It's possible that some heroes have still not completely eradicated all the electronic bugs accumulated during the course of the adventure. If Balance has not been dealt with, he and two hired thugs track the heroes into the caves within d4 hours of the heroes' entrance. The perfect time for the conclusion of this particular plot thread is when Balance and his cronies confront the heroes just as they attempt to make peaceful contact with the Tribe (see M15). If the heroes have eradicated the bugs, Balance (or some similar AHD black-ops operative, if Balance is out of the picture) tracks the heroes to the cave entrance. However, without the aid of the electronic bugs, Agent Balance only manages to arrive in time to attack the heroes as they exit the test plot.

Small Building (Bunkhouse)

The small building visible behind the greenhouse is the living quarters for the scientists permanently assigned to the project. The small house contains six separate bedrooms, three bathrooms, and a common living and kitchen area. Nothing of exceptional interest can be found in the research barracks.

Greenhouse

Half of this building is glass-sided and contains all the tools, soil grades and fertilizers, juvenile plants, and supplies normally associated with a large greenhouse, including basic facilities for botanical research and germination terrariums. The "interesting" portion of the building is not glassed, has no windows, and is only accessible through the large exterior garage door and a regular door.

The garage door is padlocked from the outside, while the regular door is locked from the inside. Either lock yields to a successful Manipulation–*lockpick* check.

The large space beyond the door is mostly open. Several metallic nets hang on a well immediately above several large lockers. A long bench is

Botanists Christine Hill & Nelson Kuniansky

Level 5 Tech Ops

STR	8	[0]	INT	12	[+1]
DEX	11	[+1]	WIL	10	[0]
CON	10		PER	9	

Durability: 10/10/5/5   Action Check: 13+/12/6/3
Move: sprint 18, run 12, walk 4   # Actions: 2
Reaction: Ordinary/2   Last Resorts: 1

Attacks
Unarmed*   4/2/1   d4s/d4+1s/d4+2s
    * +d4 base situation die

Defenses
+1 resistance modifier vs. ranged attacks
+1 INT modifier vs. encounter skills

Skills
Athletics [8]–*climb [9], jump [9]*; Vehicle [11]–*land [13]*; Movement [10]–*swim [11]*; Stamina [10]; Survival [10]; Knowledge [12]–*first aid [13]; language: English [15]*; Life [12]–*botany [15], biology [13]*; Physical [12]–*chemistry [13]*; Animal Handling [10]; Awareness [10]–*intuition [11], perception [12]*; Investigate [10]–*research [12]*; Resolve [10]; Interaction [9].

Gear
Watch, cell phone, laptop computer

cluttered with bits of rock, small bones, and broken arrowheads. A loading dock is built into the rear wall, in which the metallic sliding doors of an elevator are visible.

This chamber serves as the entry to the cavern system discovered by AHD almost fifty years ago; however, the modernization of access, including the elevator, was only upgraded in the last three years.

This chamber is usually empty, and the heroes find it so when they first enter it. A stake-out of the elevator and the building in general reveals that the two spelunker-researchers (see M0 below) only return to the surface for 8 out of every 24 hours, during which time they eat, sleep, and shower in the nearby bunkhouse before descending to their research sites once more. If the heroes encounter these researchers aboveground, refer to M0 below for statistics and attitudes.

Arrowheads, fragments of clay pottery, and bones lie on the countertop, along with several small brushes, a microscope, and microscopy supplies. A successful Social Science–*anthropology* check identifies the items as artifacts reminiscent of the archaic peoples of North America. Several Early Archaic (8000–6000 B.C.) sites exist in Mammoth Cave National Park. It was near the end of the Late Archaic period that Indians began exploring Mammoth Cave and other caves in the area, collecting minerals they found.

Strangely, while some items are quite old, some are obviously of recent manufacture.

The lockers contain spelunking equipment, including ten full sets of helmets and helmet lights, kneepads, long pants and over-the-ankle boots (with lug or deeply treaded soles), gloves, harnesses and associated climbing gear (including nylon rope, a plethora of carabiners, friction plates, and many types of "friends"), and wet suits. A successful Investigate–*search* check at a +1 step penalty also reveals a small box of dynamite in the very back and bottom of one of the lockers.

The two metallic nets are useful both as standard nets and also as mobile Faraday cages, capable of suppressing the field-effect ability that some mothmen possess. A net launcher is racked below the nets, as well as two "ketch-all poles," occasionally used to catch mothmen.

The elevator is large, and contains only two buttons. One button is labeled "Surface." The other is labeled "Pellucidar." The elevator shaft plunges 162 meters into the earth and opens onto M0 below.

Dynamite
Bundle of three sticks (LI/G), complete with blasting cap; Demolition–*set explosives* to use; d8+4w (out to 2 meters)/d8w (out to 3.5 meters)/d12s (out to 7 meters).

Ketch-All Poles
Essentially the polearm version of the garrote, this long pole has a grip and reel at one end, and a large loop of nylon cord at the other. It is used to ensnare stray animals and prevent them from running away or attacking.

The victim's Dexterity resistance modifier is lowered by 1, 2, or 3 steps, based on the result of the user's skill check (Ordinary, Good, or Amazing). Note that if the ketch-all's user manages to get it around the throat of a breathing creature (an Amazing success) and decides to pull the cord as tight as possible, it acts as a strangulation attack (see the "Strangulation" sidebar in Chapter 3 in the *Gamemaster Guide*).

Melee–*bludgeon*; Accuracy +1; Personal; LI/O

Net Launcher
A bulky, compressed air rifle with a conical muzzle that throws a weighted net when fired. The launcher only holds one net at a time; reloading requires d4 rounds. A target trapped in a net cannot move except at by crawling (half normal walk rate), has a Dexterity resistance modifier 2 steps lower than normal, and has a +2 step penalty to actions requiring physical movement. Netted targets may escape by wriggling free (a Dexterity feat check requiring a full round) or breaking free (a Strength feat check with a +2 step penalty, requiring only a single action).

Heavy–*direct*; range 2/4/8; LI/O

Mammoth Cave National Park

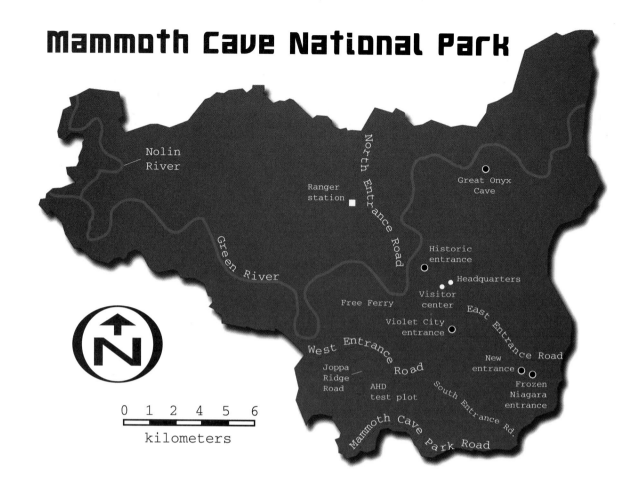

Spelunking

Refer to this section for aspects of realistic caving, if you do not personally have such experience. Heroes with Athletics–*climb* may make Knowledge skill checks at a +1 step penalty to determine if they have general spelunking knowledge and/or specific knowledge of cave formations.

Locomotion: Unlike show caves, which usually contain lighted and paved passages, wild caves are more difficult to navigate. Although many passages allow the caver to walk upright, it is also not uncommon to have to climb, squirm, crawl, or sometimes swim to move from place to place in a wild cave. While the heroes explore the caverns codenamed "Pellucidar," they will be subjected to all these environments, as is noted in each specific entry.

Light and Sound: Except for flashlights that heroes may bring into the caves, the environment is absolutely dark. Coupled with the tomblike silence of most passages, absolute darkness can unnerve even the most experienced caver. Thus, extra lights and batteries are important for any cave trip. The surrounding rock is also a very good insulator of sounds emitted even from relatively nearby passages. The rock is far too thick to allow cell phones or GPS receivers to function at this depth.

Environment: The underground temperature is constant year-round at roughly 54° F (12° C). Some passages are dry as bone, while others are slick with condensation and seepage from surface rivers and lakes, or even underground lakes and aquifers.

Cave Life: Although things are different in deeper portions of the earth, the part of Pellucidar where the heroes must journey teems with life. The associated Mammoth Cave, of which this cave system is a part, holds the world's most diverse cave ecosystem. Approximately 130 forms of life exist in the cave, but most are quite small. Some use the cave only as a haven, while others are such specialized cave dwellers that they can live nowhere else, because they have adapted exclusively to life in the darkness.

Natural animals the heroes are most likely to run into, as keyed into each room entry, include bats, crickets (and cricket droppings and eggs, which are important for delivering energy to the ecosystem), eyeless cavefish and crayfish, springfish, salamanders, pack rats, flies, gnats, and spiders. Additional connections to the surface also make it possible that heroes could encounter occasional raccoons, frogs, or even human cavers.

Speleothems: As water and time enable the removal of limestone and the formation of cave passages, so too do they enable the deposition of "cave decorations" called speleothems. These decorations include the following types:

Gypsum flowers: White to gold flowerlike structures that seem to ooze and curl from the wall, ceiling, and floor much like icing from a cake decorator's nozzle.

Soda straws: Thin-walled hollow tubes about 5 millimeters in diameter. They form as water runs through their centers and deposits rings of calcite around the tips of the formations.

New rank benefit: Athletics–*climb*

▶ At rank 3, this specialty skill encompasses the study of caves, cave formations, and cave conditions, as well as the ability to navigate caves. The skill includes a facility with associated caving equipment, and also allows one with this skill to provide aid to someone without this skill in a cave-related incident, on a successful check at a +1 step penalty. This aid, at the very least, gives a –1 step bonus to Athletics and related skill checks by novices moving through difficult cave passages.

Stalactites: Deposits grow down from the ceiling, forming as mineral layers are carried along by water flowing over the outside of soda straws. They form after the centers of the hollow soda straws become plugged.

Stalagmites: Deposits grow up from the floor in places where mineral-laden water drips from above. Stalagmites are often, but not always, found beneath stalactites. They have flat or rounded tops as compared to the carrot-shaped stalactites.

Columns: These form when stalactites and stalagmites meet.

Boxwork: Exposed crystal fins "growing" in boxlike patterns.

Flowstone: Past water flow spread deposition in thin sheets on walls and over ledges, creating flowstone, often in banded hues of brown and orange, like icing.

Rimstone: A type of flowstone, rimstone creates small dams and pools with upraised ledges. Sometimes whole series of rimstone dams and pools form.

Cave coral or *Popcorn:* Irregular clusters or rough knobs of crystalline calcium carbonate. They build up on walls and existing formations.

Draperies: When past drops of mineral-laden water trickle down the undersides of inclined ceilings, deposits form in lines that fold and curl as if they were drapes or curtains.

Argonite: Argonite formations look like nothing so much as ice crystals, and are sometimes called "frostwork."

Mammoth Cave Keyed Entries

When heroes decide that only a physical investigation of the facility will suffice, refer to the Pellucidar map on the back interior cover, keyed to the entries below.

Individual entries are usually keyed to multiple areas of the cave system. Each specific entry lists up to five important elements for each area. In most cases, the elements called out in the list are described more fully under the "Spelunking" header above. In this way, most of the entries act as the instruction framework that allows you to put together the descriptive pieces previously provided. Unless specifically noted otherwise, temperature and other universal features apply in each cave area. The elements listed under each entry include:

Access: This header describes the mode of locomotion required to pass into or through the area. In certain cases, the entry indicates that each hero must make an Athletics–*climb* check (or Athletics check). Failure indicates that d4 additional minutes must be spent in navigating the area. A Critical Failure could mean that a hero has become wedged into a crevice, fallen from a height (GM applies appropriate falling damage, based on size of area), or some other appropriate outcome.

Formations: A simple listing of cave formations in the specific area (described in "Spelunking" above).

Contents: Calls out litter, minor cave life (described in "Spelunking"), or other interesting items.

Encounter: Lists major cave life, and special encounters.

Development: If any; varies by specifics of contents and encounter.

M0. Anchor Room

Access: Easy.

Formations: An arrow drawn on the ceiling has the appearance of an anchor. The arrow points toward the northern tunnel.

Contents: Elevator, cement-leveled floor, and five small wooden stands cluttered with camp gear and arrowheads. Small crickets chirp in the corners during any period of inactivity.

The camp gear includes a Coleman stove and about twenty cans of Campbell's Steak 'n' Potato Soup. The stands contain several small arrowheads, apparently collected from the cave.

Encounter: The two researchers based in the caves, Ken Allgier and Mike Wiles, spend most of their time exploring, looking for alternate routes to access the area AHD is calling "Pellucidar." Heroes who wait in this area encounter the researchers leaving this chamber at around 9 P.M. or entering the caverns at 5 A.M. Between 9 P.M. and 5 A.M., Ken and Mike are topside getting some shuteye in the barracks. Otherwise, the heroes have a 20% cumulative chance to run into the two researchers with each new keyed area they encounter while down in the caves.

Development: When heroes first meet Ken and Mike down in the caves, the two researchers have no reason to believe the heroes are anything other than a special team sent by AHD. After all, why else would they be down here? In fact, their first question to the heroes is, "Any news on the cure?" Ken and Mike have a lot of knowledge useful to the heroes. If the spokesperson for the heroes makes a successful Deception–*bluff* check, the researchers answer freely. If the bluff is revealed either by party action, hostility, or the arrival of Agent Balance, the heroes may still be able to get the information once they have subdued the suddenly violent researchers, who are loyal to AHD first, and morality and science second.

Ken and Mike know the following:

- "We managed to get a few xenoforms wandering around in this cave system right after we rigged the elevator a few years ago. Unfortunately, they retreated into deeper caverns and sealed off all the known entry points with rockfalls, except for one weird black wall (M10). Since then, several teams have worked on and off down here to try to capture another xenoform, or at least explore a new tunnel access. So far, no luck."

- "Yeah, this is where we collected the *C. cnidarae* specimens. The xenoforms weren't too happy about that."

- "No one knows how long the xenoforms have lived down here, but it's a good bet that they've been down here longer than humans have been in North America. We've accumulated a lot of evidence that an amazingly robust cave ecosystem exists deeper,

Ken Allgier & Mike Wiles

Level 6 Tech Ops

STR	9	[0]		INT	12	[+1]
DEX	11	[+1]		WIL	10	[0]
CON	11			PER	8	

Durability: 11/11/6/6   Action Check: 13+/12/6/3

Move: sprint 18, run 12, walk 4   #Actions: 2

Reaction: Ordinary/2   Last Resorts: 1

Attacks

Ketch-all pole	10/5/2	LI/O	see text
Net launcher	10/5/2	LI/O	see text
Range 2/4/8			

Defenses

+1 resistance modifier vs. ranged attacks

+1 INT modifier vs. encounter skills

Skills

Athletics [9]–*climb [12], jump [10]*; Melee [9]–*bludgeon [10]*; Heavy [9]–*direct [10]*; Vehicle [11]–*land [13]*; Movement [10]–*swim [11]*; Stamina [11]; Survival [11]; Knowledge [12]–*first aid [13]; language: English [15]*; Life [12]–*biology [13]*; Physical [12]–*chemistry [13], geology [13]*; Animal Handling [10]; Awareness [10]–*intuition [11], perception [11]*; Investigate [10]–*research [12]*; Resolve [10]; Interaction [8].

Gear

Watch, cell phone, laptop computer, spelunking equipment, ketch-all pole, net launcher

---

somehow able to replenish oxygen and trophic levels with only limited access to the surface."

- "There must be connection to Mammoth Cave proper, 'cause we get caver traffic every so often. Poor saps." (Ken and Mike are charged with keeping the cave a secret, and so deal violently with obvious cavers, throwing their remains in the Bone Pit, M7, which is the fate of any hero who perishes here.)

M1. Frosted

Access: Easy.

Formations: White and brown flowstone covers the walls of the passage.

Contents: Crickets and gnats.

M2. Constricted

Access: Tunnel narrows, requiring an Athletics–climb check to pass.

Formations: Flowstone, stalagmites, columns.

Contents: A few cigarette butts, spiders, gnats.

M3. Flowers

Access: Moderate climb, requiring an Athletics–*climb* check at a +2 step penalty to pass.

Formations: Gypsum flowers, soda straws, stalagmites, columns.

Contents: None.

M4. Overland

Access: A real climb, requiring an Athletics–*climb* check at a +3 step penalty to pass.

Formations: Draperies.

Contents: Spiders, spider webs, plus d4 arrowhead artifacts with successful Investigate–*search* check.

M5. Pooled

Access: Easy.

Formations: Rimstone (surrounding small pool of water), soda straws, stalagmites, stalactites, columns.

Contents: Eyeless crayfish and springfish in a pool with deeper connections than is at first obvious (all M5 chambers are connected and accessible via wet suits and scuba gear, but this is not known by the researchers).

M6. Big Squeeze

Access: Tunnel narrows to a fissure that looks unpassable by those unfamiliar with caving. Requires a successful Athletics–*climb* check at a +1 step penalty to pass.

Formations: Cave coral, gypsum flowers, flowstone.

Contents: A few bats, crickets, and gnats.

M7. Bone Pit

Access: Easy.

Formations: Popcorn, argonite.

Contents: A big pit in the center of the chamber. The pit is 9 meters deep, and a faint charnel odor arises from it. Strong flashlights reveal bones, backpacks, and smashed caving equipment.

Development: Cavers from Mammoth Cave National Park who have found new tunnels leading into this area have been disposed of by AHD watchdogs over the years, their disappearances covered up by high-level AHD politicking when necessary. A prolonged search of the pit reveals many gnats, crickets, and other pests, as well as the remains of twelve people and their smashed equipment. No identifying information remains with the bodies. No cavers have found their way here in the last few years because of the mothmen's efforts to completely seal up all access to the outside world.

M8. Animal Cracker Room

Access: Easy.

Formations: Argonite, draperies.

Contents: The ceiling in this room looks like a box of broken animal crackers.

Encounters: d4 pack rats. Uncovering the nest (with a successful Investigate–*search* check) reveals a lighter, string, several really old arrowheads, and one very new arrowhead, on which are painted two large red dots.

M9. Cave Paintings

Access: Easy.

Formations: Boxwork.

Contents: Very old and faint pictures are painted on the wall, in a style most would associate with "caveman art." A successful Social Science–*anthropology* check reveals that these paintings strongly resemble the work of the Archaic peoples living in the area (on the surface) between three thousand and six thousand years ago; see the Mammoth Cave listing in the Lexicon for more information.

M10. Haunted Wall

Access: Easy.

Formations: Flowstone, stalactites (Investigate–*search* check reveals faint depressions in the form of "angel wings" on the bases of many of the stalactites).

Contents: A wall of matte-black substance blocks the northeast tunnel. It might be stone, and it is at least that hard. Dynamite cannot destroy the wall, and a successful Demolitions–*set explosives* check reveals such an attempt would collapse this entire chamber permanently.

Encounter: A bound venom spirit (see the "Venom Spirit" spell in the DARK•MATTER *Campaign Book*) strikes at the first hero to touch the wall. It stays its attack at the sight of the Kwakiutl Mask; otherwise, the spirit flares with greenish light for a moment as it attacks, then fades. The victim must make a Resolve—*physical resolve* check or succumb. An affected victim takes 1 point of fatigue damage at once, and another 1 point every 4 hours on subsequent failed checks; these points cannot be recovered while the spell is in effect. An Amazing success on any of these Resolve checks ends the effect. When all fatigue points are lost, the victim falls into a coma (treat as Terminally Ill). While unconscious, the victim dreams of a vast underground space called the Third Corner of the World, inhabited by fantastic creatures.

Development: Heroes who produce the Kwakiutl Mask and reveal its inner face or who beat upon the Manitou Drum succeed in breaching the barrier, which fades away like mist. Other FX abilities may also crack the wall, at the GM's discretion. As the barrier gives way, a violent rush of wind literally screams from the orifice, knocking all heroes who fail a Resolve–*physical resolve* check to the ground and inflicting d4s.

The wind slowly abates over 10 minutes. An Athletics–*climb* check or Physical Science–*geology* check reveals that the cave wind is created by temperature differences between the outer and interior passageways. This causes a "chimney effect." The incredible blast of wind indicates that the area sealed off behind the barrier must be unbelievably huge—perhaps several thousand kilometers of cave passages. Unless this area is resealed, the secret entrance owned by AHD exhibits "breathing" characteristics every morning and night, which was how they found the cavern in the first place, before the mothmen sealed up this and other access points.

At the GM's option, heroes with appropriate FX abilities may also be able to breach the barrier, which is configured to recognize such workings as signs of the Tribe and therefore allow passage.

M11. Lamprey Room

Access: Easy (assuming the barrier in M10 is breached).

Formations: Argonite; two large geodes in this room resemble the mouths of lampreys.

Contents: Cave paintings, like those found in chambers M9, with two differences. First, the paintings cover this room from floor to ceiling, and second, many of them are vibrant and sharp, as if created in the last several years. However, the same style is evident between the oldest and newest. The newer scenes are sharp enough to reveal figures. Some figures are sticklike hunters, chasing down fantastical creatures (including amoebalike blobs). Many of the stick hunters seem to be wearing flaring capes, or have wings.

Development: An Investigate–*search* success reveals a few more arrowheads—some very new with two red dots painted on each—and a human skull with a sharp hole all the way through. A Medical Science–*forensics* check indicates that death probably occurred from an arrow strike, and the skull is only a few years old.

M12. Argonite Mummies

Access: Easy.

Formations: Draperies, argonite frostwork covering "columns," which on second glance are something altogether different.

Contents: Several bright red crickets dot the terrain here. The "frosted" columns are easy to identify after just a few seconds' study: They are people so long dead that cave deposition has coated their bodies in a filigree of delicate gypsum and other minerals. A combination of the chill air and preserving mineral deposition has "mummified" these bodies. Each chamber keyed to this entry contains 2d4 stone burials. Simple observation reveals racial characteristics similar to modern-day native Americans. A successful Social Science–*anthropology* check indicates that the bodies are most likely remnants of Archaic peoples, making these preserved forms up to 4,000 years old.

A central dolmen in each of these chambers also contains very old symbology, in the form of cave paintings. Should the heroes have any way of deciphering the symbology (requiring a success on a Social Science–*anthropology* check at a +3 step penalty, or some other check deemed appropriate by the GM), the symbology can be translated as: "The Earth is my mother; on her bosom I will rest."

M13. Child of the Beast

Access: Easy.

Formations: Draperies, argonite "mummies."

Contents: No natural lifeforms of any type (but see "Encounter"), otherwise as M12.

Encounter: A cnidocyte currently resides in this chamber, though it is initially dormant and spread out upon one of the walls, looking for all the world like a natural "drapery" formation. If the heroes disturb it by entering this chamber, it slowly coalesces into its amoebalike shape and attacks from the shadow. Refer to the secondary cnidocyte stats presented in Act Two, Scene Two, P12.

M14. Animate Argonite

Access: Easy.

Formations: Draperies, argonite "mummies."

Contents: No natural lifeforms of any type (but see "Encounter"), otherwise as M12. A successful Awareness–*perception* check reveals the very, very faint sounds of drums and pipes, which echo in this chamber with ghostly faintness, rising, and falling again to silence. (The sound actually echoes from M15, but from this chamber, the source is impossible to locate.)

Encounter: The three mummies in this chamber do not rest quietly. Since AHD's invasion a few years ago, the Tribe has called upon its shamans for protection. These argonite mummies are infused with magic, and if any living creature (not natural to the cave) enters the chamber, the sharp report of cracking rock precedes their clumsy but deadly animation. Heroes who retreat from this chamber are left alone, unless they retreat down the tunnel leading toward M15, in which case the mummies give chase. If the heroes can make it to M15, the shamans there may call off the mummies' attack.

The argonite mummies fight until destroyed, at which point they

Animate Argonite Mummies

STR	12	[+1]	INT	5	[–1]
DEX	8	[0]	WIL	12	[+1]
CON	13		PER	5	

Durability: 13/13/7/7

Action check: 10+/9/4/2

Move: sprint 20, run 12, walk 4

#Actions: 3

Reaction Score: Marginal/1

Last Resorts: 0

Attacks

Unarmed	14/7/3	d6+2s/d6+2w/d6+4w	LI/O

Defenses

+1 resistance modifier vs. melee attacks
+1 WIL resistance modifier vs. encounter skills
Argonite deposits: d4+2 (LI), d6 (HI), d4 (En)

Skills

Athletics [12]–*climb [13], jump [14]*; Unarmed [12]–*brawl [14]*; Stealth [8]–*sneak [12]*; Stamina [13]–*endurance [20], resist pain [15]*; Awareness [12].

fall into little rocky pieces. Should any Child of the Beast (cnidocyte) enter the chamber, the mummies preferentially attack it over the heroes.

M15. Gathering of Shamans

Access: Easy. During initial approach, music emanating from this chamber becomes more distinct.

Formations: Draperies, stalactites, stalagmites, cave coral.

Contents: Bright and vivid cave paintings, obviously very new.

Encounter: A smokeless fire burns in a central pit, around which are huddled six figures in what appear at first glance like long cloaks. All the figures are employing pipes, drums, or rattles to create a beautifully haunting song. The musicians cease playing simultaneously as the first hero approaches. In fact, the figures are all mothman shamans, and the "cloaks" are their furled wings.

Six important shamans of the Tribe (what the mothmen call themselves) are gathered in this chamber, the doorway to the Third Corner of the World (their name for vast cavernous spaces belowground, what AHD calls Pellucidar). The mothmen silently study the heroes until the heroes initiate contact. The mothmen recognize that the heroes are working against their enemies (AHD) and do not wish to fight, but should the heroes' xenophobia get the best of them, they'll find the mothmen quite a match. Heroes with the Kwakiutl Mask can initiate conversation. Failing that, one of the shamans uses its irregular knowledge of the English language to speak with the heroes.

The shamans relay the following under questioning:

- "We lead the Tribe. The Tribe has long lived here, at the edge of the Third Corner of the World. The Third Corner is a living world that exists below yours. We hunt the periphery, content in our ways, and have done so since before the humans came, the first of your kind. We befriended them. We taught them some of our skills, and both our peoples profited from the contact. But that's all long ago now. Your people do not now embrace the ways of the Tribe, nor do you wish to."

- "Many things walk the Third Corner of the World. Even the Tribe doesn't hunt too deeply. Strange, appalling creatures haunt those dim lands. One season several lifetimes ago, the Summoning Winds blew strong, and the Beast emerged from the Deep in terrible power—the earth shuddered as the Beast passed into being. Our greatest warriors and shamans died in the attempt to turn it back through its Doorway. In the end we succeeded, but only with a Pact."

- "The Pact had many parts, but the most important commanded the entity to return whence it came. But the Tribe was compromised, for the Pact also called for the Tribe's inaction. The Tribe cannot cause harm to the Beast or its kin. Unbeknownst to us, the Beast's mere presence spawned a taint, which remained behind: the Children of the Beast, also called the Formless, though the Formless were only the least of the danger left by the insidious Beast."

- "The Beast secretly shed a portion of itself. Infused with the power of the Realm Beyond, this threat bides its time and has only recently revealed itself, perhaps in response to actions of your people or the rise of the <incomprehensible>. But, we have held it back, barely. The Tribe calls this horror the Residuum."

GM Note: The mothmen know of the rising Dark Tide and its

effects on the world, but they have a hard time articulating the concepts to nonmothmen.

- "The Residuum is a remnant of the Beast. Though only a part of the whole, it is steeped in powers of the Realm Beyond, and it knows only evil."

- "From the time of the Pact to now, the Tribe has dedicated itself to a war of holding. Though we may not directly end the threat, we can contain it, and hold it back from infecting the upper world. We have restrained this evil for generations, though little acknowledgment or thanks have we received from the other races that inhabit this world. Should we compromise the Pact, the Beast may return, but should we fail in our attempt to fence in the Residuum, ruin also follows."

- "The minor taint that we call the Children of the Beast is a formless evil. As is the way of things, evil calls to evil. Not so long ago, some of your people heeded that call. Despite our attempts to prevent it, they were contaminated by the Children's evil, as all your people are susceptible to its touch. They were also fascinated by its power. Selfish, they stole outlying members of the Tribe away. They wanted the secret of our immunity to the Children's contamination. That is something they shall not have. We have sealed ourselves in, so that they may not find us. But the Summoning Winds are blowing once more, and the Residuum moves from its long slumber. It reaches for the surface."

- "We shamans are gathered here now, preparing for a confluence long foreseen. Your arrival here, or those much like you, was expected. We perceive your need, but we have a need greater yet, which you can fulfill. Strike against the Residuum, which the Pact forbids us. Be our clenched fist, and we will provide you with what you seek."

The mothmen want the heroes to destroy their bane, called the Residuum. Normally, the plethora of supernatural powers at the Residuum's command would blast the heroes' minds and bodies in an eyeblink. However, the shamans intend to shield the heroes from these effects using a variation of their *ghost dance* ability, though they remain unable to take a direct part in the conflict due to the mysterious Pact. If the heroes are successful, the shamans provide a cure to their *C. cnidarae* affliction (see below).

If the heroes decide they want no part of such an arrangement, the shamans are quiet, and then one points toward the tunnel whence the heroes entered. Reluctant heroes are escorted out (there is no Pact stopping the shamans and up to one hundred additional mothmen from harming human heroes).

Heroes who agree to the mothmen's request for aid are treated better. The mothmen indicate that no time is to be lost; the confluence approaches. One shaman (and only one) removes its Ghost Vest and loans it to the heroes, who can give it to whomever they wish. The shaman indicates that the vest is a boon to a warrior. They can also heal any character stricken by the venom spirit in area M10. The mothmen return to their eerie melody, but with obvious added fervor—a shaman informs the heroes that the Residuum will recognize the new cadence as a challenge, and attempt to rush the mothmen's guardianship of the cavern's exit. That's when the PCs must strike!

The Residuum Cometh

The heroes have 10 minutes to prepare, if they so choose, once the shamans begin their song of challenge meant to lure the Residuum. As the clock ticks away, a shaman warns the heroes to stay within sight of the shaman during the conflict, or lose the benefit of their protective influence. Thus, heroes are confined to the ledge. Though they may overlook M16 and the lights of the cliff dwellings, the ravine below is lost in ominous darkness, which swallows a flashlight's beam like an ember in a dark sea.

When the attack comes, it is sudden:

Rivulets of darkness, like effluvium from a polluted stream, flow up and over the rocky ledge. The rivulets herald the arrival of a terrible monstrosity. Dripping shadows, the horror itself is transparent. It pulsates with sick vigor, releasing a vomitous stench. Arcane whispers scratch at the back of your mind, but are immediately drowned out by the shamans' song. Undeterred, the Residuum gropes forward like nothing so much as a severed hand . . . a hand the size of a bulldozer.

Like a tertiary cnidocyte, the Residuum has formed from a cast-off portion of a larger creature. However, unlike the cnidocytes the heroes have encountered, this creature formed from an entity of which *C. cnidarae* is but a "natural" part. From this fact, and from its incredible size, the Residuum has arcane abilities that dwarf any offered by the human mind. However, through training and dedication, the mothmen shamans can adjust their *ghost dance* ability to counter these FX effects. Thus, the heroes have a fighting chance—while they remain in sight of the shamans. For its first action, the Residuum attempts to *dissolve* one of the heroes; when this fails to work, the creature realizes that the mothmen's power protects the heroes. In between attacking the PCs, it attempts to reach the shamans to end their chant, and the heroes' only hope of victory is to make sure that doesn't happen.

During the conflict, the shamans remain seated in their circle, shielding the heroes from foul sorceries. Meanwhile, the ledges and windows of the glittering cliff dwelling across the gorge fill up with the silhouettes of hundreds of mothmen, who watch the entire conflict in stony silence.

Aftermath: If the heroes fall or flee before the Residuum, failure is its own reward. If the heroes triumph, the shamans play a song in their honor, while the mothmen of the cliff dwellings continue to watch. The shamans say:

"For your service to the Tribe and to life itself, we give you the gift you desire, the method to cleanse yourself of evil influence."

Ghost Vest

This vestlike garment is made from the leather of some indeterminate creature. The armholes are particularly wide, and each extend over a portion of the upper back of the vest. Strange symbols are dyed over the entire fabric, most of which are too stylized to understand.

Powers: The power of the Ghost Vest is great. Each time the wearer is struck by a physical force (LI/HI/En) strong enough to inflict damage, the wearer makes a Will feat check. If successful, the wearer takes no damage from the attack. On a failure, the wearer takes damage as normal. On each successful use of the Vest, one of the symbols smokes and disappears. The Vest begins with d6 such symbols (providing a maximum of that same number of uses).

One of the shamans produces a small woven-fiber bag, tossing it to the nearest hero. The bag is filled with pungent, leaflike herbs. If smoked or ingested as a tea, the leaves completely and immediately cure the affected individual of *C. cnidarae* infection. The bag has enough doses for seven cures. At the GM's option, these herbs can also be effective in healing all but the most virulent illnesses. The heroes may keep the Ghost Vest, as well.

- If heroes wish, one of the shamans takes the heroes to look out over the Third Corner of the World (M16), but only briefly. The shamans indicate that those of the upper world and those of the Third Corner do not mix out of long tradition.
- After the heroes have been accorded the honors their victory deserves, and perhaps have weathered Agent Balance's final attack (see "Wrap-up" below), the shamans inform the heroes that they must return quickly to the surface. The shamans are preparing another ceremony that cannot wait; it is their intention to reseal the FX barrier (at M10). When the heroes oblige, they begin to hear the fluting music of the shamans again as they depart. And as they pass back through M10, the dark barrier again springs into place. If the heroes wish to remain in the mothmen's good graces, they'd best not open the barrier again.

M16. Pellucidar

The cavern opens up above and below, and to each side. Hundreds of tiny, firelike lights provide dim illumination. The light reveals a dome at least 30 meters above, and a canyon below it running approximately 100 meters to the northwest, before a bend hides the rest of its extent from view. The sound of a river gurgles up from the canyon floor below, at least 75 meters away. The opposite side of the canyon is the source of the light, as it twinkles in sparkling profusion from the windows of a majestic cliff dwelling.

The mothmen of this Tribe live in this canyon, which stretches many kilometers deeper into the earth, before connecting upon a space of vast size. They call this vast subterranean space the Third Corner of the World. However, the mothmen spend most of their time in the canyonlike approach, and subsidiary tunnels that lead away from it. The canyon is rich in life, some familiar and some unfamiliar, with which the mothmen exist in harmony. Occasionally great warriors head into the Third Corner, and sometimes terrible monsters and unfriendly races emerge from it, but generally the mothmen leave the vast space alone.

An exploration and explanation of even the canyon of the Tribe, let alone the Third Corner, goes far beyond the scope of this adventure. In any case, the heroes are urged back to the surface, and this cosmology only becomes important to those GMs who wish to develop it. Note that as the shamans mentioned, the Tribe is not the only colony of mothmen on earth, and even if the heroes never venture again to the canyon of the Tribe, or into the Third Corner, they may still encounter these otherworldly creatures.

Wrap-up: Act Two, Scene Three

As this scene draws to a close, the heroes head back to the surface. If the heroes have peaceably interacted with the mothmen, retrieved their gifts, and agreed to return to the surface, the music of the shamans haunts their footsteps the entire way back.

Tribe Shamans (mothmen)

STR	9	[0]	INT	7	[0]
DEX	11	[+1]	WIL	12	[+1]
CON	8		PER	8	

Durability: 8/8/4/4   Action check: 11+/10/5/2
Move: sprint 20, run 12, walk 4, fly 40   #Actions: 2
Reaction Score: Ordinary/2   Last Resorts: 1
FX Energy Points: 6

Attacks

Wing strike	5/2/1	d4s/d4+1s/d4+2s	LI/O
Talons	11/5/2	d4s/d6w/d6+1w	LI/O

Defenses
+1 resistance modifier vs. ranged attacks
+1 WIL resistance modifier vs. encounter skills
Light Sensitivity: +1/+2/+3 step penalty in Ordinary/Good/Amazing light, respectively
Ghost Vest   see sidebar

Skills
Athletics [9]–*climb [10], throw [10]*; Unarmed [9]–*brawl [11]*; Acrobatics [11]–*fall [12], flight [14]*; Stealth [11]; Stamina [8]; Knowledge [7]; Life–*xenology [9]*; Awareness [12]–*intuition [14]*; Lore [12]–*occult [15]*; Interaction [8].

FX Skills
Faith FX (Shamanism)–*dreamwalking [13], ghost dance [13], hunter's stare [13], trance visions [13], venom spirit [13].*

Gear
Ghost Vest, rattle, pipe, drum, medicine pouch

Residuum

STR	20	INT	17
DEX	12	WIL	17
CON	20	PER	10

Durability: 20/20/10/10   Action check: 17+/16/8/4
Move: undulate 10   #Actions: 4
Reaction Score: Good/3   Last Resorts: 1
FX Energy Points: 8

Attacks

Bludgeon* (×2)   10/5/2   d6+2w/d8+4w/d6+1m   HI/O

* +d4 base situation die.

** Nematocyst effects also apply. If any hero has taken direct damage from the Residuum, the victim must make a Constitution feat check at a +1 step penalty. Those who fail the check become infected with *C. cnidarae*; refer to the sidebar "*C. cnidarae* Contamination" in Act One, Scene One for onset time and symptoms.

Simultaneous FX Attacks (prevented by shamans)

Dissolve*	18/9/4	2d6+2w/2d8+2w/2d4m	En/O
Mind Blast	18/9/4	3d4+2s/3d6+2s/3d8+2s	En/O

* As *pyrokinetics* in effect, but in appearance, victim is overrun with rivulets of darkness and dissolved as damage is taken.

Defenses

+2 resistance modifier vs. melee attacks
–2 resistance modifier vs. ranged attacks
Immune to psionic attack
Armor: d6+2 (LI), d6+2 (HI), d6+2 (En)

Special: Only completely killed if burned. "Slain" Residuum otherwise recovers full health in 10 days.

Skills

Stealth [15]–*hide [18]*; Stamina [20]–*endurance [20]*; Awareness [17]–*intuition [18], perception [18]*; Resolve [17]–*physical [18], mental [18]*.

Heroes concerned for the continued secret of the mothmen and concerned with AHD's presence may use the dynamite in the nearby metal locker to collapse the elevator tunnel. If the heroes have not had their final encounter with Agent Balance yet, this is a good time for it, especially if Balance didn't intrude on the investigators' contact with the shamans. Balance's first ploy is diplomatic: He asks, "Did you find the cure? We can make a deal, you know. . . ." Of course, Balance double-crosses the heroes once the cure is in his hand, should the heroes be so foolish to trust him. Either way, Balance confronts the party with two thugs and two handlers. (See statistics for Balance and handlers in Wrap-up: Act One, Scene Three and statistics for thugs in Act One, Scene One.) This time, Balance doesn't back down—he's out for the heroes' blood.

Final Wrap

In the days following the adventure, interested heroes note telltale signs of their success, as portrayed by the following headlines:

- Lower Kentucky Experiences Mag. 2 Quake—"No One Hurt."
- AHD Pharmaceuticals Victim of Random Arson—"A Total Loss."
- Counseling for AHD Workers Suffering from Memory Loss.
- Point Pleasant Springwheel Regatta Biggest Ever—"Over 40,000 Attendants."

Awards: Award each hero 1 achievement point for each of the scenes the heroes completed to your satisfaction. You may decide to award these points as the heroes complete each scene. If the heroes distinguished themselves, or otherwise added to the overall experience of the adventure, award them 1 additional achievement point. Additionally, award 1 bonus point to each hero if Balance is dealt with for good, 1 bonus point if they freed the mothman of Point Pleasant from its curse, and 2 bonus points if the Residuum is permanently killed.

Conclusion: If all goes well, the caverns are sealed with an FX barrier, and possibly even partially collapsed (if the heroes use the dynamite provided). AHD Pharmaceuticals' body of research, samples, and ability to garner new test samples have been destroyed. The safety of both the heroes and the general populace has been assured for a while longer, at least as regards this particular threat. Moreover, the Tribe returns to its peaceful meditations in its secret subterranean demesne, indebted to the heroes for their aid.

In less than perfect circumstances, AHD Pharmaceuticals' parent company AHD, Inc. has a record of the heroes' activities against it. In a worse scenario (for the PCs), Agent Balance remains alive and a potential future threat (the GM may prefer this scenario). However, even in the worst case, AHD has other important issues to deal with, and Balance is too important an asset to waste on acts of pure vengeance. Still, Balance may remain a useful adversary for the GM to pull out in future adventures when the heroes least expect it.

Coincidentally, the heroes have the favor of the Tribe (assuming the heroes dealt amicably with the shamans). Should the heroes ever run into mothmen in later adventures, they are treated as friends, even if the heroes do not possess the Kwakiutl Mask. However, the door swings both ways—should the mothmen of the Tribe require aid, they contact the heroes in visions and dreams. The Tribe has many enemies, and their knowledge of the modern world is more complete than anyone suspects. Should another threat materialize in the Third Corner of the World or from another Doorway, the heroes may wake from dusty dreams of terror to find their visions a reality.